A Christmas Song

THE GHOST OF CHRISTMAS
YET TO COME

A Christmas Song
by The Ghost of Christmas Yet to Come
Copyright 2015

Cover design and interior formatting by Tugboat Design

NEW CASTLE, RHODE ISLAND

To begin with, Ebenezer Scrooge was dead. That one thing you must remember, or you will not appreciate the wonder that follows.

Thomas G. Pemblin parked his car. He closed the garage door and walked around the side of his house. It wasn't his normal route inside, but as he was carrying a Christmas gift for each of his children, he wanted to make sure he wasn't seen.

He had three of them, children, that is. And there was no doubt that each gift he'd selected would bring a tickle of joy when opened. After all, Pemblin knew his children well, and joy was all he wanted for them during this time of year. He slipped the smallest gift into his coat pocket and tucked the remaining two under his arm. The undisturbed snow crunched beneath his feet.

Pemblin was a sturdy man. Hard working and educated. From good stock on all fronts, one might say. He wasn't given to anger, unbridled passions, or too much of the bottle. He sought understanding in contentions, always assuming that he was the one who didn't see clearly, and thus made himself a student of all things. A stalwart and happy man. A trusted man.

He spoke little, except when he had to, and tended mostly to his own business. A likable and good man. An honest man.

But a fool in his own regard.

'Twas Christmas Eve. A special night in most homes, but doubly special in the home of Thomas G. Pemblin, as it was also the birthday of his eldest child. Gordon, who answered to the affectionate nickname Gordi, was ten years old.

Pemblin made it a point to celebrate the seasons of the year and birthdays of his children. He didn't insult his child by merging holiday with birthday. Likewise, he didn't diminish the holiday by merging it with birthday. Gordi's birthday and Christmas, one right after the other. A double celebration. A man of means, Pemblin could afford to do it.

December the twenty-fourth had always been a happy day in the Pemblin household. But on this, Gordi's tenth birthday, something different happened.

It would forever change Thomas G. Pemblin.

"Merry Christmas, Tom!"

Over the picket fence that divided their property, Pemblin saw Brian Hartwick shoveling snow in his driveway. The Hartwicks had been neighbors to the Pemblins for all thirteen years of his life in New Castle. Neighbors, for sure. And friendly, to be sure. But not quite the friends Thomas wished they could be. No bad blood, no unkind words or discord. Just neighbors and nothing more. It made him a little sad.

"Merry Christmas to you, too, Brian." Pemblin stopped

and rearranged the packages under his arm. "Shoveling snow on Christmas Eve?" he teased. "Surely you can think of something better to do tonight."

Brian stuck his shovel in the snow, rested a foot on the metal spade and leaned toward Pemblin. He twisted his mouth and nose in as ugly and mean a face as his pleasant features would allow. He pointed a finger at Thomas and spoke in a raspy voice. "Humbug! You keep Christmas in your way and I'll keep it in mine." He laughed at his own joke.

Thomas returned the laughter. "Well said. I'm off to celebrate Gordi's birthday with the family. Then someone else's birthday tomorrow." He winked.

Brian began shoveling again. "Have a good evening, Tom. Tell Gordi happy birthday and give everyone else a merry Christmas."

THE BIRTHDAY

Thomas walked on the stone path that crossed his yard and led to the front door. He'd taken three steps when the wind arose so strongly that he wasn't able to put his foot back on the ground. He hung suspended in the air, kept upright on one leg by the strength of the wind. It was like he was in the middle of a hurricane. He looked to his left and right, expecting to see the carnage inflicted by the terrible storm, but there was none.

Before he found a scientific explanation for the funnel of wind that held him aloft, a voice penetrated his ears.

"Tonight, Thomas G. Pemblin. I come tonight."

No sooner had he heard the words then the tempest died, and his step connected shakily with the ground. Not willing to move just yet, he lingered. "Tonight?"

Had he been a simpler man, Thomas would have entertained thoughts of Santa coming down the chimney. After all, it was Christmas Eve, and who else should he expect? He had plenty of faith in the season, and perhaps his mind should have drifted to He whose season it was, but he knew he wasn't important enough to receive a house call from the Astronomer Royal.

No. Neither of these would come to him.

The voice he'd heard, though soft on the wind, was unfamiliar and felt threatening. Perhaps unpleasantness was intended. An unwelcome visit? He shuddered and put such nonsense from his mind. He wiped his feet on the doormat and smiled at the wreath which hung over the entry way. "Merry Christmas, wreath."

He entered his house and was attacked by the smell of so many good things. Scented candles mixed with freshly baked pies, a smoked ham dressed with bacon; a Christmas turkey was probably being prepared for cooking. Somewhere there was a cake with candles waiting to be lit.

If Thomas was good, then Mrs. Pemblin was perfect. Intelligent, determined and kindly, she put her many talents toward that which she loved most: family and home. She used her talents well and whole-heartedly.

And so it was that after a stupendous dinner, the five members of the Pemblin family, Mr. and Mrs. Pemblin, Gordi, and the twins Jillian and Lisa, all gathered round the table in a song of "Happy Birthday."

Pemblin handed his son a small rectangular package. It sparkled in red metallic wrapping. "Happy Birthday, son."

"Ooooo," the twins sang in unison as the package twinkled in the light.

Gordi accepted it with a smile. His eager fingers tore at the package until it was unwrapped. He stared at his present.

"What is it?" Jillian asked, trying to look over her sister's shoulder.

"A book?" Gordi asked, sounding uncertain. His expression changed from anxious delight to confusion. His forehead crinkled downward, and the edges of his mouth curled in a disbelieving smile. He looked at his father and shook his head. "Really? A book, Dad?"

"A wonderful book!" Mr. Pemblin countered Gordi's disbelief with hopeless optimism. "One of my favorites, in fact. It's perfect for this time of year. Read the cover so everyone knows what it is." He smiled encouragingly. "Go on. Read the cover."

Gordi read aloud. "*A Christmas Carol*, by Charles Dickens." His eyes fell to the floor. "This is stupid. It's a book. I thought I was getting my own phone." He folded his arms and looked like he was going to cry.

Pemblin looked like he'd miscalculated a jump and was falling to his death. "Well, son, this book is special." His eyes darted to his wife for reassurance. "I'd hoped that every December you could read this and remember how magical this time of year is, and in turn remember how special I think you are." He smiled lovingly.

"Every year!" Gordi looked offended. "You want me to read this book every year? Seems like a waste of time, Dad. *You're* the one who always says put your time on what matters most." He slumped lower in the chair. "I said I wanted my own phone. All my friends have one." He tossed the book onto the table. "No thanks."

Mr. and Mrs. Pemblin exchanged looks. In most things

they were in complete alignment. However, on this occasion they were not. Mrs. Pemblin was about to make Gordi's tenth birthday his last. Being a gentle man, and always trusting in the goodness of his opposition, Mr. Pemblin extinguished her fury with calm eyes and a soft tone.

"I can see how I misjudged, Gordi." His voice was soothing. "Girls," Pemblin directed, "please grab the blue package from my overcoat pocket. It's hanging by the front door." He'd slipped the extra gift into his pocket before he came in the house that night. His intention was to put it under the tree when all the kids were in bed. He was glad he had it ready.

The twins had watched the birthday exchange silently. Not knowing exactly what was wrong and neither possessing the maturity to understand Gordon's dissonance, they jumped from their chairs and retrieved the blue box for their father.

"Here you are, Gordi," Pemblin said as he handed the package to his son. "Happy Birthday."

Once again, eager fingers tore at wrapping paper. This time a smile won out. "A phone!" Gordi pumped his fist in triumph. "I knew it. Thanks, Dad." He dove from the chair and gave Pemblin a giant hug. "You're the best."

An Unexpected Visitor

Pemblin ate the Christmas cookies that were thoughtfully left by Lisa and Jillian. He knew they were for Santa, so they were actually for him. He laughed about how wonderful they thought Santa was. Because *really* it meant they thought *he* was wonderful.

And how could he forget the reindeer food? Couldn't forget Rudolph and the rest of the crew. He smiled to himself as he buried the cinnamon-sprinkled oats deep in the trash. He had to make sure Lisa or Jillian would never find it.

With everyone in bed and all things ready for the mighty day that is Christmas, Pemblin crawled in bed next to his wife.

On most days, only the best of feelings existed between Mr. and Mrs. Pemblin. However, on this night there was a poignant staleness in the air. Thomas was about to ask Mrs. Pemblin how she was, but she spoke first.

"It's not right," she said softly.

"What's not right, Denise?" Thomas asked. He cleared his throat. "I've taken care of everything." He clicked his tongue and squinted his eyes, like he was trying to remember something he'd forgotten to do. "Milk and cookies are gone, the reindeer food has been disposed of and all the presents are under the tree. What did we forget?"

She sat up in the bed and looked at him, her cheeks flashing a little red. "Our better judgment, I'd say."

Mr. Pemblin blinked in surprise. "What are you talking about? It's Christmas Eve, dear. Let your heart be light," he sang, and smiled. "Look outside." He pointed to the window. "Snow is falling, we are warm inside, and our children sleep with sugar plum fairies dancing through their dreams. Tomorrow they will wake to Santa's gifts, and it will be a marvelous day." He breathed in satisfaction. "Merry Christmas."

"Gordi!" She looked at him incredulously. "How can you ignore his behavior tonight and then reward him with a new phone? If I didn't want to have a good evening or a good tomorrow, I would have cut into his arrogance like fire through snow." She folded her arms. "It wasn't right, and we did nothing."

"Sweetheart," Pemblin soothed. "He's ten years old and still a child. And the best behaved child I've ever seen. Shouldn't he be entitled to what he wants?" Pemblin bit his lip as he considered the way Gordi snubbed his birthday present. "I was disappointed, but I shouldn't be surprised. I hoped the book would mean something to him later in life. I shouldn't have looked that far ahead, I guess." He shrugged. "Oh well. I'm glad I had an extra gift nearby. He'll have one less tomorrow morning, but he'll be fine."

"The gift was beautiful, Thomas. It's not you I'm worried

about. It's Gordi." She exhaled heavily. "I've half a mind to take that phone and flush it down the toilet."

Pemblin lovingly laughed at her exasperation. "I want to be good to our children in all circumstances. Give Gordi the benefit of the doubt." He looked at Mrs. Pemblin, but she didn't return his gaze. "Darling, let's see how it turns out. I'm confident he will correct himself."

She snorted. "Did you ever, in your life, receive a gift the way your son did tonight?" She shook her head emphatically. "Did you every treat your father with that kind of disrespect?"

Pemblin thought. "Well, no. Not intentionally."

"No way and not a chance." Mrs. Pemblin was emphatic. "For the sake of Christmas, I will calm down. However, I am fully expectant that you, the father of this house, will find both an explanation and a solution for Gordi's behavior. I will hold you responsible," she huffed. "There, I've said my piece and will say no more. But the next time I witness entitlement like that, I will answer it in my own way. Probably with a stick."

Pemblin leaned across the bed and kissed her cheek. "Thank you, my dear. Merry Christmas."

Sleep had taken all but one. Mr. Pemblin lay on his back with his eyes closed. He should be asleep by now. Christmas morning and excited children would come all too soon. For Pemblin, rest was an essential ingredient for a good day.

But something was stirring his brain. Two somethings, in fact.

First was the admonition of Mrs. Pemblin. It was fresh in his mind, as it was the last thing spoken to him. "I will hold you responsible," she'd said. *Hold him responsible.* For what? Gordi's outburst? How would she hold him responsible? He immediately thought of success or failure.

The second something in his mind was the mysterious wind that had accosted him on his way to the front door. "I come tonight," the wind had said. At least it sounded like the wind . . . if the wind could talk. But Pemblin knew the wind could not talk.

Restless, he got out of bed for a drink. Pemblin stepped into the hallway, and the door behind him closed. He froze.

The hallway was blocked by a man. His skin was pale like a white melon, the lips under his pointed and skinny nose tight and thin. In the man's eyes, Pemblin saw a strange twinkle, like starlight trapped in black orbs.

The man's clothes were not of modern time. He wore a thick, cotton-like three-piece suit with four large buttons on the front and a dove tail coat that hung to the back of his knees. The collar around his neck-tie was stark white and high around his chin. On top of his head sat a long top hat with a red ribbon and a holly flower wrapped around the brim.

"What are you staring at?" the man said in an old-timey English accent. "I told you I would come, did I not?" Pemblin was paralyzed with fear. "Don't look so surprised," the stranger said. "I did announce myself." He shook his finger accusingly. "Don't deny it."

Pemblin, who had not said a word or moved except to shake and tremble, opened his mouth to speak but could not.

The man in the hallway observed Pemblin's condition. "Oh, it's fear you feel. I understand fear. On this night, you may have reason yet to fear, but not right now. Not with me."

"Wh-wh-who are you?" Pemblin asked, his voice no louder than a whisper.

"Me?" the man asked. "I am Ebenezer Scrooge."

THE WONDERS OF CHRISTMAS EVE

The Ebenezer Scrooge that had slipped into legend was, in fact, dead. And had been for centuries. Therefore, Pemblin could only conclude one thing: the man who stood before him was insane. A trespasser who somehow entered the house and intended to butcher them while they slept. The murderously insane have no regard for anything, not even the sacredness of Christmas. In his mind's eye, Pemblin saw his children dead in their beds. The morbid image gave life to his limbs.

He shouted at the top of his lungs, trying to alert Mrs. Pemblin. She could call the police. He reached for the man's arms, expecting a fight, but the man didn't move. Instead of resistance, Pemblin touched nothing. He passed straight through the man, as if there was nothing there.

He turned around to face the demon, his hands in a defensive position. "My children, what have you done to them?"

"Good gracious, Mr. Pemblin. They are sleeping in their beds. Should they be anywhere else?"

"No games!" Pemblin demanded. "What do you want?"

"Calm down, Mr. Pemblin," Scrooge soothed. "You'll

give yourself the pox if you don't."

Pemblin shouted to his wife again. "Denise! Wake up! Call the police!"

"You can shout as loud as you wish." Scrooge shrugged. "She won't wake."

Pemblin waited to hear shuffling around in the room. Any second now and Mrs. Pemblin would immerge and ask what the ruckus was. It was silent. He put his hand over his forehead like he was taking his own temperature. "I'm dreaming," he said.

Scrooge shook his head dismissively. "Humbug."

"Why won't she wake? She doesn't sleep through anything. If this were real, she'd be up in an instant." He rubbed his eyes. "Definitely a dream."

"If you say so," Scrooge agreed, non-committedly.

"What else could it be?" Pemblin wasn't talking to Scrooge as much as he was talking to himself.

Scrooge turned his nose upward, and the corners of his mouth lifted into a smile. He pulled down the brim of his hat like he was taking a bow. "Magic," he said as he winked. "Christmas magic, in fact. That's what else it could be."

Pemblin shook his finger, unconvinced. "And you." He pointed. "I can see and hear you, but can't touch you." He grinned knowingly. "You're not really here, are you?" He laughed crazily. "A dream."

"I say again, Mr. Pemblin. I said I would come. Here I am. It was my wind that held you aloft this evening. It is I who fill this home with magic that only you should see and hear me. And if you do not calm yourself and let me work my purpose, it is I who shall witness your damnation."

"Damnation?"

"See here," Scrooge confirmed. "Damnation, indeed." He shook a long bony finger in Pemblin's face. "And not just yours."

Pemblin was beyond bewilderment. "Not just my own damnation?" he repeated slowly. His forehead crinkled in confusion.

"Indeed," Scrooge huffed.

Pemblin considered the implications of damnation. His mind was about to travel a path of unending questions, but he snapped back into reality. There was an apparition in his hallway. Ghost!

"Wait just a minute!" Pemblin waved his hands in the air like he was a referee calling for a time-out. "You're not a man. I walked through you." Inflections in his voice betrayed uncertainty. "What are you?"

"As I've said, my name in life was Ebenezer Scrooge. It was I who lived as a miser, until a Christmas miracle gave me the chance to correct my course. Tonight, on this hallowed Christmas Eve, I give warning to you. Take heed of my words.

"For on this night, you shall be visited by three spirits."

"Visited by three spirits," Pemblin repeated. A light clicked on in his head. "*A Christmas Carol* with Ebenezer Scrooge." Pemblin felt like he'd solved a riddle. "That's it." He snapped a finger. "I'm having a psychological reaction to Gordi snubbing my gift." He chuckled, sounding crazier than before. "Charles Dickens. Makes perfect sense." Thomas pretended Scrooge wasn't there. He turned around like he was going back to his room.

"Thomas G. Pemblin!" Scrooge bellowed, his eyes turning into fire. The house shook, and Pemblin thought a hole would appear and swallow them up. He faced the ghost that called himself Scrooge.

"Tonight!" Scrooge's voice was deep and menacing.

"Please," Pemblin said as he shielded his face. "I'm listening."

"You shall be entertained by three spirits. Each has a message patterned after your need. Should you ignore them, you risk the consequences that shall befall you and yours."

Pemblin's eyes were as big as tea cups. "Ebenezer Scrooge," he said, trying to sound as congenial as his frightened tongue would allow, "I hope you will forgive me, but. . . . Well, um."

"Stop mumbling," Scrooge demanded. "If you've something to say, then say it."

Pemblin took a breath. "I'm not unaware of my faults, but I think I live well. I mean, I'm not perfect, but I'm not a miser like you were." He put his hands up defensively to shield himself from Scrooges impending wrath. Through the cracks in his arms, he saw that Scrooge had not moved. "No offense. It's just that, this hardly seems necessary. I've never spurned the spirit of Christmas like you did."

Scrooge stared at Pemblin. "By the stars in the sky. What are you trying to say?"

Pemblin cleared his throat. "I mean no offense, Mr. Scrooge."

"Call me Ebenezer."

Pemblin smiled. "Okay, Ebenezer. Of all the people that

need change or Christmas intervention, why me? Three spirits to correct how I feel about Christmas? I love Christmas."

Scrooge removed his hat and placed it over his heart. The eyes under his bushy eyebrows looked sad, and his smile faltered. Observing the change in Scrooge's countenance, Pemblin feared he'd been unkind. "I didn't mean to hurt your feelings, Ebenezer. Your reformation is legend to the world. Everybody loves you, myself included. I only wonder why, of all the souls you could visit, you chose me?"

Scrooge put his hat back over his head, his smile and eyes returned to their sparkly selves, and he began to chuckle. It was soft and pleasant, and the sound of it brought comfort to Pemblin. And yet, the chuckle crescendoed into a strong and hearty laugh, and that laughter grew in strength until it became the sound of thunder. Pemblin closed his eyes and covered his ears, frightened that he'd be blasted by sound waves or go deaf from the tremendous booming.

In an instant, the sound stopped. Pemblin opened his eyes, and he was alone in the hallway. Ebenezer Scrooge was gone.

THE GHOST OF CHRISTMAS PAST

Pemblin sat on the edge of his bed. He looked at his wife, amazed she'd slept through Scrooge's tirade. It made the house shake and had caused him to cower.

Christmas magic? Ebenezer Scrooge. Damnation?

"A dream," he said to himself. "Just a dream." He chuckled lightly, but his mirth was short lived. He covered his mouth to stop himself from screaming. Unless his eyes were tricking him, a top hat sat on the floor beneath his window-sill. It was the same one he'd seen on Scrooge's head minutes ago, a red ribbon with a holly blossom wrapped around the brim.

Pemblin shook his head from side to side. He hoped the motion would convince him that he wasn't seeing the hat, or that whatever screw was loose in his brain would set itself right.

No. The hat wasn't on the floor. No. He hadn't talked with Ebenezer Scrooge. He closed his eyes and pushed it all from his mind. No. No and No. He forced his breathing back to normal and uncovered his mouth. He needed to fall asleep before he proved he was crazy.

Pemblin stretched out on the bed. *Closed. Closed. Closed. Keep your eyes closed.* Any second now, and the warmth of sleep would overtake him.

And warmth did overtake him, but it was not the warmth of sleep. Light penetrated his eyelids, like a flashlight had been switched on and pointed at his head. With the light came heat, small at first, but in seconds it encompassed his body until he felt uncomfortably warm. Fearing that he might be ignoring a fire in his bedroom, he opened his eyes.

To his surprise, there was a fire. A flame billowed above the floor, moving back and forth as if following the patterns of wind. The flame touched nothing, but gave light to every corner of the room, like noon on a summer's day.

Pemblin sat upright, mystified by the phenomenon. Inside the fiery light was a tiny man, no longer than Pemblin's own arm. Or maybe the man was the fire. He wasn't sure.

The rectangular body wafted to and fro, like the moving surface of golden water. Its arms were long and muscular, shining amber against florescent flame. The face was a perfect sphere wrapped in flame with a long tail of light where hair should have been. In one hand, the creature held a large golden thimble. He placed it over his head, and the light that filled the room diminished. The spirit glowed like a giant candle.

Pemblin wiped his eyes. He'd seen many strange things in to short a time. He needed to get his eyes checked. He reached back and shoved his wife. She didn't stir, so he shook her harder. "Denise!"

"She won't wake," the personage said. The voice was like

the flicker of fire moving in the wind; strong on some conso-
nants but weak on others. It sounded like he was far away,
then close, then far away.

"Why not?" Pemblin asked, thinking he already knew the
answer.

"Christmas magic," the flame said, sounding like it shouted
from miles away. To Pemblin's ears it was just a whisper.

Pemblin sighed. *Christmas magic again.*

He'd hoped his conversation with Scrooge had been a
dream, a Christmas delusion. Yet, the image before him was
proof that he had spoken with the ancient miser. "Are you
one of the spirits Ebenezer Scrooge told me to expect?"

"I am here at Ebenezer's request," the spirit said. "Yet a
much greater design than Ebenezer is in motion." The spirit
pointed a finger at Pemblin. "To which you are a central
figure."

Pemblin was a sober man in most things, and especially
in things pertaining to himself. He couldn't imagine a plan
that would require him to play a central role. Or if he was
the center of it, he thought it must not be a very good plan.
"Central figure, how?" he asked.

"I am the Ghost of Christmas Past and have come to talk
of days gone by. The future is not mine to reveal."

Pemblin looked upon the Ghost of Christmas Past. He
recalled the role this spirit played in Scrooge's redemption.
If his memory of the legend was right, it was this ghost that
took Scrooge back to his childhood days. It was this ghost
that showed Scrooge his lost love Belle, his betrothed who
he abandoned for the pursuit of wealth. Pemblin distinctly

remembered the shame that Scrooge felt when faced with the poor choices of his youth. Suddenly, he was afraid of the Ghost of Christmas Past. Pemblin could not remember what shadows he had buried away in his mind, what heart aches he had caused and chosen to forget. He did not want to visit his past.

"Spirit," Pemblin spoke pensively, "Are you that same ghost who escorted Scrooge to his childhood days?"

The spirit smiled proudly. "I am he."

Pemblin looked at the spirit expectantly. "You did much to influence Scrooge. Are we going to re-visit my childhood and my heartaches also?" he probed.

The spirit smiled brightly. "You know the reformation of Ebenezer Scrooge. His heart turned so fully that he has become the forerunner to the Spirits of Christmas. As I came to Scrooge in his hour of need, so it is that I come to you. Not for thy salvation alone, but the salvation of the season." The spirit bowed his head. "We will visit your past."

Pemblin considered this. *Why was he hosting the spirits of Christmas?* He didn't see the purpose of it. How could his heart turn more towards that which he already loved? Christmas was already his favorite time of year. What change could be made in his heart?

At the same time, he couldn't explain his own acceptance of what was happening to him. Maybe it was that he'd already failed to end the hallucinations, or maybe he was too tired to fight the impossibility of what he saw. Perhaps his mind was twisted by fatigue, but here he was conversing with the Ghost of Christmas's past.

Dickens and Scrooge and Spirits and Christmas magic. It was all impossible.

Yet, as he saw no harm in it, and believing he could not control it, he decided to embrace whatever experiences he should have, whether in his mind or out of it.

He looked at his miraculously still sleeping wife. "If I go with you, will my family be protected?"

"Indeed they shall be. Protected by Christmas magic." As the spirit spoke, his figure moved about like fire in the wind. Here a second and then nowhere, a millisecond later somewhere else. "You go willingly," the spirit observed. "I sense the goodness of your heart, Thomas G. Pemblin."

Pemblin saw an opportunity to exploit the perception of his own goodness. "If I'm good, then why are we doing this?" He loved Christmas and had always tried to keep it well. He didn't believe he needed a change of heart. "How can I experience a change of heart like Scrooge did?"

The spirit did not answer, but extended his arm. "Take my hand that you may fly. Don't let go, lest you fall and forget."

Cautiously, Pemblin grabbed the tiny hand and flew into the air. He hovered like a puppet with invisible strings. "I'm not practiced in balance, Spirit." He tried to steady himself in the air, but there was nothing he could cling to besides the Ghost of Christmas Past. "I'm a large fellow, and you are so small. I won't drag us down?"

"One man can sink the memories of Christmas, but I have the strength of a million glorious Christmases past. The memories I contain will lift multitudes. "Come," the spirit invited, "tonight we visit that which has already been." The spirit waved his hand at the window, and it slid open, allowing a few snowflakes to float into the room.

Like threading a needle, Pemblin maneuvered through the window until his entire body was outside. Had he not been fifty feet above the ground, he would have considered it a wonderful Christmas night. The large flakes of snow and the white earth below looked pristine. As it was, he'd never been fond of heights and after one look down, he decided not to look again.

"Spirit?" His voice quivered as he tried to ignore the distance to the ground.

"Speak," the spirit invited.

"As I've said, I'm familiar with the role you played in Scrooge's redemption. The story is legend in my day."

"So you say."

"On that fateful night of Scrooge's repentance, you pulled him along just as you pull me now. I know the account well. In the sky, he saw the souls of men and women robed with the chains of their deeds. After death, are we bound to our actions in life?"

"It is so," the spirit confirmed. "Even now, the dead are before my eyes."

"Why can't I see them?" Pemblin asked. "Scrooge did, and they caused great fear in his heart. Shouldn't I see them too?"

"Are you the same as Ebenezer Scrooge? The experiences meant for him are not meant for you. Know this, Thomas G. Pemblin, the dead, both small and great, are all around us. And yes, they carry the chains of their deeds. Fear not,

Pemblin. You shall yet see chains and those wrapped in them. Look forward, for we visit that which is past."

The snow around them stopped falling and hung in the air as if painted on the canvas of sky. In a terrible burst of speed, Pemblin and the spirit catapulted through clouds and stars until their path was a crystal ball of light.

The sky disappeared and they were standing on firm ground. A long yellow school bus slowed to a stop in front of worn down, two-story apartments. The bus pulled away, leaving a small pack of children which scattered in every direction.

Pemblin searched excitedly, anxious to see his younger self. "Where are we? I don't know this place." He examined the decaying buildings, confusion replacing his excitement. "Spirit, I've never lived in apartments."

Pemblin's mind was searching. "Hey. And when are we?" He'd accepted the fact that he wouldn't experience exactly what Scrooge had. But by the look of the clothes people wore and the cars on the streets, for all Pemblin knew it could be yesterday.

"One score years ago."

"Twenty years ago?" Pemblin questioned.

"Yes," the spirit confirmed. "You will not recognize it, Thomas. This is not a Christmas memory of yours." The spirit spoke as if instructing a child. "We shall yet be in your past, but tonight is not meant for you alone. There are others that need salvation also. Open your eyes that you may see. Open your heart that you may feel."

Pemblin felt a twinge of shame for being self-centered.

"Others need salvation?" He didn't understand the context. How could anything they were doing bring salvation to anyone?

"Salvation, indeed," the spirit said. "See there, those two children?" He pointed his long arm. Two boys waited for traffic to clear, then crossed the street. Their path took them right by Pemblin.

"Hi, boys," Pemblin greeted.

"They can't see or hear you," the spirit instructed. "We are shadows within memories and not truly here. You need only watch and listen."

"Oh, yeah. Right." Pemblin put his hands in his pajama pockets.

One boy spoke emphatically while the other stared at the ground, eyes filled with horror.

"I'm telling you, Alvi. Santa Claus is not real. Think about it. You've asked for a billion things and only got what can be bought in a store. There is no workshop with elves." The words festered in momentary silence. "And the Thompsons, every year they all get the same white shirts and black socks, the same bowl of candy and a new basketball."

"They all love basketball," Alvi interjected.

"Brett Henderson never gets anything because his family has no money. He's lucky if he gets a good dinner for Christmas."

"Yeah, so what does that mean?" Alvi asked defensively.

"That means," the tiny educator enunciated, "Santa is a sham. Why would he give presents to some people and not to others? Brett's just as good as you and me. If Santa existed, he'd get Brett something too, and everyone else on the planet."

Alvi's eyes looked for answers. "Well, not everyone celebrates Christmas."

"So what. We do, and I know Santa doesn't exist. No elves, no workshop, no reindeer, no Santa."

Alvi crossed his arms around his chest, and moisture filled his eyes. "You don't know."

The kid put his hands in his pockets and kicked at a rock. He looked deflated, like he was upset by his own reasoning. "I looked in my dad's closet and saw a bunch of toys. On top of them was my letter to Santa. And my sister's. Mom and Dad just say they send the letters, but they don't. They just buy the toys from a store. It's all fake."

"Hi, boys."

Pemblin turned around. A man approached and playfully ran a hand over Alvi's head. "How was school today?"

They looked at the ground, not completely done with their conversation. The man noticed the unhappy looks on their faces. "Whoa. Hey, guys. What's the matter? You both look like you're about to cry."

Neither of the boys responded.

The man looked at them suspiciously. "Tomorrow is Christmas Eve. You should be excited. And if Christmas doesn't cheer you up," the man teased, "there's no school for two weeks."

Alvi looked up at the man, moisture in his eyes. "Dad, Brian says Santa isn't real." He fought to keep the tears from falling. "I keep telling him Santa *is* real, but he doesn't believe me."

Pemblin guffawed. "Tough situation. I'd like to see him be an honest man after handling this."

The man looked at the boys, his jaw muscles working as he ground his teeth. He got down on one knee and looked at Alvi face to face. "You're a smart kid. Maybe even the smartest I know. I'm lucky to be your dad." He put a hand on Alvi's shoulder. "Let me ask you a question." He reached up and tapped Brian's arm. "You too, Brian. Listen up. If there is no Santa Claus, does that mean there is no Christmas?"

Alvi met his father's eyes. "Well, no."

He stood up and reached for his son's hand. "Come on, Alvi. Your mother's waiting for us. Merry Christmas, Brian," the man said over his shoulder. "Tell your folks I said hello." Alvi and his father walked hand-in-hand toward the apartments.

As Pemblin watched them walk away, he thought about the question. "If there is no Santa Claus, does that mean there is no Christmas?" Something about it conveyed an unconventional wisdom. "Tell me, spirit, who is that man?"

"You may yet know more of him," the spirit said. "Just a man. Take my hand."

Pemblin clasped the spirit's hand, and they flew into the clouds. The white swirling vapors disappeared, and Pemblin was standing in a small, square room. It resembled a hospital room, but it wasn't clean enough to actually be one. The baseboards were smeared with old dirt and splotches of mold, and the windows had permanent streak marks that made them look gray instead of clear. The print design on the linoleum floor had faded from decades of foot traffic, but around the edges of the room the old pattern was still visible.

An old and emaciated woman lay on a bed, her eyes empty and her breath shallow. Except for the woman, a rickety chair and a calendar on the wall, the room was empty.

Pemblin glanced at the calendar. Across the top in bold print it read, "July." Sunlight poured through the dirty open window, and dozens of flies had flown into the room. The heat was oppressive.

"Spirit, it's not December." He gestured to the calendar.

"I know the times." The spirit pointed to the open doorway. "Is the spirit of Christmas meant only for December?"

A woman walked through the door. Red hair hung to the center of her back, and she carried a thin book. Her dress was straight and simple, an ordinary flower design printed on it. Her shoes showed heavy scars of wear, like years had passed since they needed replacement. She grabbed the chair and set it close to the bed.

Pemblin recognized her youthful face. "Mom?" He was surprised to see her in such a place.

She sat down, took the woman's hand, and rubbed it. "Hi, Victoria," she said. "How are you today?"

The woman in bed rolled to face her visitor. The corners of her mouth formed a smile. "Melodee." Her voice was weak and broken. "Happy to see you again."

Melodee smiled back. "We have to finish the book." She held it up. "See?" She pinched the last few pages together. "That's all we have left."

"What about when we finish?" The old woman looked

concerned.

"Oh, there are lots of books we need to get through. Pay attention, now. This is the best part." She began to read.

"Spirit," Pemblin asked. "Who is the woman in bed?"

"Do you not know her?"

Pemblin took a closer look at her face, and shook his head. "I don't think I know her."

"Hers," the spirit said, "is the face of loneliness."

"I mean *that* woman, Spirit. Who is she and why is mother visiting her?" Pemblin scanned the room, looking for something that would bring back a memory. "She never told me about this place or Victoria. At least that I can remember."

"Why should she tell you?" The spirit wafted to and fro. "Would you take away the silent satisfaction of helping without acknowledgment?"

"But who is Victoria to my mother?"

"No one," the spirit replied. "And everyone."

Melodee held Victoria's hand as she read. "How long did she visit her?"

The spirit pointed to the calendar. The month had changed from July to December. "Until the end of her days."

The light in the room dimmed, and the stale heat gave way to piercing cold. Pemblin's mother stood by the empty bed in a thick winter coat. There was no sign of Victoria. "Good bye, my friend." Her breath was visible against the cold. Melodee swept her hand lovingly along the bed.

"I don't understand," Pemblin said. "Why would she visit someone like this and never speak of it?"

"I say again, why should she speak of it?" The Spirit

removed the thimble that covered his head, and light exploded from the top of it. It was like a lighthouse beacon, shooting a thick beam of brilliant light. The small room could hardly contain the illumination.

Pemblin shielded his eyes. "That is really bright."

"This is the spirit of Christmas. It is the light that forever ignites my burning wick. It exists because selfless kindness exists."

The light washed over Pemblin's skin. It reflected off his face and hands, wove around his hair and moved against him like waves of water on the beach. Suddenly, Pemblin was happy like he never had been before. "What is this that I feel? Such a strong sensation."

"My light is the love of mankind. That is what you feel." The spirit pointed. "There are more."

"More?"

"Yes." The spirit flickered like a flame about to be blown out by the wind. And then, in one colossal boom, light exploded from every angle of his tiny body, shooting beams from his head to his toes. Brilliant white strands blasted the room to pieces. Pemblin thought he would go blind, but the brightness faded, and he was no longer in the hospital room. "Look," the spirit urged.

Pemblin saw his mother again. Her once youthful face and flashing red hair now showed signs of maturity. Her smooth and fair skin had aged, the wrinkles around her eyes and mouth more pronounced. She took a baby from a crib and placed him on carpeted floor. The baby neither smiled or cried or acknowledged her touch. His eyes, though alive, were stagnant.

"Spirit," Pemblin observed. "I don't know much about babies, but that one doesn't look right to me."

"Yea," Christmas Past agreed. "This baby will die from his malady. He can feel hunger, but do nothing to express it. He can experience love, but do nothing to show it in return." The spirits mouth curled downward in an exaggerated frown. "Indeed. His light is dim."

Pemblin watched his mother massage the baby's head with the tips of her fingers. She moved her hand down his face, stroking his cheeks and nose. After several minutes, she began to rub the arms and then the stomach, followed by the legs and feet.

"What is she doing?" Pemblin asked.

"What she can." The spirit put himself between Pemblin and the scene, hovering directly in front of his face. "She gave time and kindness. Both things that are free to mankind, yet there is rarely enough to be found."

"Who is the child?" Pemblin asked.

"To your mother," the spirit said, "no one." The pupils in his eyes turned into flames. "And everyone."

The spirit extended his hand to Pemblin, who sighed and took it.

Instantly they were in a spacious room decorated with musical instruments. Stacks of books and papers cluttered the floor. A man sat at a piano bench, his hands working over the keys with gentle force and strategic energy. He finished his masterpiece, folded his arms, and looked at the ceiling like he was thinking.

"Wonderful!" Pemblin declared. "Have you ever heard anything so beautiful?"

"Look," the spirit instructed.

The man stood up, one hand covering his mouth while the other held a piece of sheet music. He paced back and forth, humming sometimes and other times singing aloud. "Oh!" he exclaimed, disappointment on his face. He threw the papers in the air. "It's not good enough!"

He kicked the piano bench and stubbed his toe. He grimaced and glanced at his watch. He gasped. "I'm going to be late!" He gathered the papers, put a long black coat over his shoulders, wrapped a scarf around his neck, and walked out the door.

"Who is this?" Pemblin asked.

"This is a man from *your* past, Mr. Pemblin." The spirit beckoned for him to follow the man.

"Mine?" Pemblin questioned, as he stepped through the door.

They followed through snowy streets, and Pemblin began to recognize the buildings. "This is my hometown, isn't it?"

The spirit smiled knowingly. "Indeed it is. Remember the man? He is rarely forgotten by those who meet him."

"No, I don't remember him." Pemblin crinkled his forehead.

They stopped at an old stone chapel with a large white steeple. A poster hung on the door. It read, "Christmas Eve Performance: Handel's Messiah, conducted by Dr. Kent H. Leslie."

"Spirit," Pemblin said, "is the man we follow Dr. Leslie?"

"The very same."

Pemblin shrugged. "I still don't remember him."

Inside the chapel, a full choir was organizing itself in a large gymnasium. Pemblin was surprised at the number of people bustling around a stage. Some were preparing instruments, wiping them down or tuning them, and others were arranging themselves into rows and columns. "There must be a hundred people up there." He pointed to the pit below the stage. "An orchestra, complete with brass and drums. Now that's an impressive ensemble."

"Indeed," the spirit agreed.

"Everyone!" Dr. Leslie yelled. "To your places. To your places, please." He positioned a box in front of the choir, stood on it, and from somewhere on his person he pulled a long, thin, white baton. He tapped it on the podium, and the room fell silent. "From the beginning," he said. He pointed the baton toward the ceiling and in one beautiful, swan-like motion, he swung it down. The orchestra began to play.

Had the music been sustenance, nothing could have tasted sweeter. The director motioned for the choir to join in. Pemblin closed his eyes and let the sound have full access to his mind.

"Stop! Stop!"

Pemblin opened his eyes to see what was wrong. The director stood with hands on his hips.

"I can't lead a sloppy choir. Not for this piece and not in this season." A few faces in the choir looked startled. Others looked annoyed. With dramatic flair, the director threw his baton into the air and it landed in the empty chairs near

Pemblin's feet. The director covered his face with his hands and shook his head like something had gone terribly wrong.

"I thought we sounded pretty good," someone said. A few people echoed the sentiment.

"Yes," the director agreed. "You sounded *pretty* good. *Pretty good.*"

"Come on," someone moaned. "I don't want to practice for three hours again. Can't we just continue?"

"Spirit," Pemblin asked. "What's wrong with the music?"

"Listen," the spirit responded.

The director regained his composure. He walked down into the chairs and retrieved his baton. Pemblin heard the words the man muttered as he passed by. "It must be perfect," the director said. "Nothing less will do."

He retook the podium. "My friends," he began, "listen to me on a personal matter, and then we can continue. I won't interrupt anymore." He paused dramatically, waiting to ensure that all eyes were on him. "I love Christmas. I love the season, and I love the meaning of it. 'Hark, the Herald angels sing,' it is written. 'Hallelujah,' we sing. 'Glory to God on the highest.' Yes." His eyes filled with emotion. "I rarely get to express my love for Him whose season it is. This one commission fills me with such pride that I've poured my soul into the arrangements.

"There are many of you, but I need you to sound like just a few." He lowered his head, trying to hide his tears. "I love you for your time. These weeks you've sacrificed your evenings. These many hours in pursuit of harmony. I love you for letting me be here with you."

He looked at the group with renewed devotion. "And I ask more of you. More time, more oneness, more Christmas Spirit. Three days stand between us and the performance that makes my life significant. Please, my friends. Thousands will come to hear you sing, and you shall wish them a merry Christmas through song. When they leave this chapel, they must feel the spirit of Christmas. 'Hallelujah' and 'Silent Night' must be on their lips and in their hearts." He tapped his chest emphatically. "I can't put it there. You can." He lifted his baton. "Now, one more time."

The room faded to blackness, and the only thing Pemblin could see was the glowing spirit, who smiled and snapped his finger. Immediately, the room was lit again and full of spectators. Instead of sitting in the audience like before, Pemblin and the spirit were at the back of the auditorium facing the now-decorated stage. Red ribbons and streamers hung from the balconies. Poinsettias and Christmas flower arrangements were everywhere.

"It looks like they're about to perform. Is it Christmas Eve?" Pemblin asked.

"It is," the spirit replied.

Pemblin looked for an empty chair but saw none. People stood along the walls and sat in the corners or leaned on the doorways. In the back of the chapel, tables were filled with Christmas cookies and bowls of Christmas punch.

"Know you now the man?" the Spirit asked. Pemblin wanted to say that he did, but he couldn't. He shook his head. The spirit pointed to the tables of treats where a young boy reached for a cookie. "And that boy, recognize him?"

Pemblin did. "Oh, spirit. Was I here on this night? That's me, isn't it?"

"Watch and listen," the spirit instructed.

Pemblin watched his child self run fingers over the cookies, obviously enthralled by the feast. "I shouldn't be doing that," he uselessly chided himself.

The director cued the symphony and chorus. As the sound filled the chapel, the young Thomas Pemblin abandoned the cookies and turned toward the music. Pemblin watched his younger self react to the melodious Christmas cannonade. As he did so, his mind filled with the senses of his youth. He remembered how the music penetrated his heart and moved him to ask questions.

Pemblin remembered.

"It was here, Spirit. It was here and it was this music. The first time I felt Christmas for myself." He laughed softly. "This is the first time I understood what Christmas really was."

"Spirit?" Pemblin looked for the Ghost of Christmas Past, but he was gone. Pemblin was back in his bedroom, alone with his sleeping wife.

THE GHOST OF CHRISTMAS PRESENT

Pemblin sat on his bed. Outside the window, he saw the snow reflecting in the moonlight. The digital clock by his bed told him it was one o'clock in the morning.

Merry Christmas.

He should be tired, but what he'd just experienced was still coursing through his veins. A *real* visit from the Ghost of Christmas Past. Somehow sleep didn't feel appropriate.

Besides, Ebenezer Scrooge foretold three visitors. And if Pemblin's night was patterned after Scrooge's Christmas Eve so long ago, next would be the Ghost of Christmas Present. Of all Christmas spirits, this was the one Pemblin wanted to see most. Large and jolly, full of laughter and all for making merry with song, good food, and drink.

Pemblin walked to the window for a closer look at the snow. He rested his hands on the window-sill and gazed at the moon, a silver backdrop for the thick flakes. In the distance, he saw the long prairie that ran behind his subdivision. Under the thick layer of snow, it looked like a sea of rolling whiteness, and then it ran into the dense pines that were the beginning of an endless forest.

He was almost lost in the view when an unfamiliar sound echoed in the night. To Pemblin's untrained ears, it sounded like the howl of a wolf. He thought he imagined it, until the howling came a second time. It was closer and louder than before, somehow ominous and cruel.

"What is this?" he said, peering through the window.

In the distance, a figure ran out of the forest. It was large like one of the trees. Its path was easy to follow as it tore through the snow, creating a frozen wake behind it. In the pale moonlight, it was hard for Pemblin to see details, but it looked like a man. He wore a cape or a giant robe, which billowed behind him as he ran against the wind. His mighty legs moved so fast that in seconds he'd traversed half the distance between Pemblin's house and the forest's edge.

The howls grew louder. Pemblin followed the sound and saw large beasts pursuing the giant. The man, who would soon be at Pemblin's front gate, was mostly naked. Except for the robe, his only clothing was a girdle around his hips.

Pemblin strained his eyes. Splotches of snow behind the man were discernably red.

Blood.

As the giant got closer he shrank, and by the time he reached the front gate, he was the size of a man. Larger than any man Pemblin had ever seen, but an acceptable size for a human. Maybe.

The man secured himself in Pemblin's front yard just in time. The wolves smashed into the metal barrier, and the fence almost collapsed under their weight. With a stick, the half-naked man poked the wolves through the fence. He taunted and jeered before he left them.

There came a knock at the door.

Pemblin couldn't let a stranger in. Not under these circumstances. The knocking came again, but it was louder and rattled the entire house. Pemblin looked at his wife, expecting to see her stir. There was no way she could sleep through the pounding.

She didn't move.

Christmas magic.

Pemblin looked out the window and saw the wolves prowling around the gate. The footprints the man had left in the yard were stained red. Pemblin's sympathy was roused. He walked down stairs and hesitantly approached the front door. The pounding was so powerful that the hinges rattled against the blows. Pemblin was surprised the door didn't break apart. He undid the latch and opened the door.

Pemblin saw large and bloody feet. Above his ankles, the man had strong and defined calves, which were riddled with teeth and claw marks. No doubt from the wolves. His calves connected to large and knobby knees that were the base for long and tenuous thighs. The muscles were clearly defined and powerful, but somehow lacked the proper proportion for someone so large. Around the man's shoulders was a thick green robe that hung low to the ground, held together by a gold chain clasped in front of his bare chest. He had a scraggly red beard, and on the top of his long red hair sat a rusty crown.

Pemblin tried not to look at the man's underwear, but he

had to. A bunch of cloth wrapped around his loins like a giant diaper. Apart from the robe, that was all the stranger wore.

He was about to ask the stranger if he wanted to come inside, but the man entered without invitation. The man carried a walking stick, which he occasionally used as a crutch. He ducked under the foyer chandelier, sniffed the air, and said, "It's this way."

Pemblin followed him into the family room. The Christmas tree shone brightly, its lights pushing back the night time darkness. Under the tree there was an impressive mound of gifts in all shapes and sizes and wrapped in a rainbow of colors. Normally Pemblin would take a moment to admire the arrangement, but his eyes were glued to the giant. He sat on the couch opposite the tree, and his large body filled the entire seat. He leaned his walking stick against the wall.

Pemblin cleared his throat. He wanted to make sure the stranger knew he was there.

"You are the man called Thomas G. Pemblin?" His voice was deep and strong, neither kind nor inviting.

"Yes," Pemblin said uncertainly.

"You can call me Spirit, Thomas G. Pemblin."

Pemblin swallowed. "You *are* the Ghost of Christmas Present?"

"I am he."

"You don't look like I expected."

"What did you expect?"

Pemblin fumbled around looking for the right words to express himself. "Um…you look skinny." He coughed and shrugged his shoulders. "Ish."

"The Ghost of Christmas Present has fallen on lean times," the spirit said. He swept his wet hair out of his face.

From somewhere, a large and ornate fireplace appeared in the living room. Giant flames spewed from its mouth, adding more light and heat to the room. The spirit held a giant goblet in his hand, which he raised to his lips and drank. He stared at the fire.

"Well," Pemblin remarked. "Are you going to say it?" He forced a smile.

The spirit took another drink. "Say what?"

"You know," Pemblin encouraged. "Like you said to Scrooge." He made his voice as deep and jolly as he could. "Come in and know me better, man!"

The spirit stared at Pemblin. "Indeed," the spirit said. "Words spoken by my brothers before me. Yet words I cannot speak." He prodded the fire with his stick and swiped his hair again. "In truth, Thomas G. Pemblin, I know not myself."

Pemblin stood awkwardly, waiting for the spirit to speak or guide him. "You are thinner than I imagined. Shouldn't you be fat?"

"My brothers were fat. Roaring fires, the Christmas Goose, turkey and ham, stuffing and wine. Breads and cheeses, apples and olives, cakes and pies. All wonderful, all cooked in the hearth and prepared for the special day. The bounties of life made the goods of Christmas. In times past, those who had shared with those who had not. I am lean because mankind's heart is lean."

The spirit prodded the fire again. "Those times are past us. That spirit which I follow is strongest of all, for the memories of Christmas Past outlive the glory of Christmas today."

"I don't believe that, Spirit," Pemblin contended. "There are many people who give to the poor and needy. Also, many companies feel it's their corporate responsibility to help the destitute." Pemblin smirked playfully, trying to lighten the mood. "Christmas Present diminished by the strength of Christmas memories. No way."

"Strength of Christmas Present?" The spirit stamped his foot on the floor. "Where is my strength and where is my glory? What dogs are at my heels? Those who freely give are but the smallest portion of those who could. Corporations are not people."

Pemblin looked at the spirit's bloody feet. "Your cuts, Spirit. Can I help with those?"

"You may yet help me, but not with these. Scratches, really."

Pemblin wasn't going to argue, but they looked like more than scratches. "Are they from the wolves?"

"Yes. They shall have their way with me in the end." He stared aimlessly at the fire. After a long silence Pemblin coughed, reminding the spirit of his presence. "And you." The spirit raised his goblet and drank. It seemed like the cup had no bottom, and for all Pemblin knew, it didn't, for the spirit continued to drink and drink but never refilled his cup. He set the mug on a wooden table that appeared from nowhere. He rose from the couch, supporting his weight with his stick. "I thank you for your hospitality, Thomas G. Pemblin. The night is growing late, and I must take my flight before more wolves arrive."

"More wolves?" Pemblin looked concerned.

"More wolves, indeed. You may yet know them before the night is through." The spirit hobbled through the room. He'd made it all the way to the front door before Pemblin called to him.

"Am I supposed to follow you?"

The spirit turned abruptly, like he was surprised or frightened. "Follow me? What on earth for? Would you be meat for the wolves as well?"

"Ebenezer Scrooge told me you would come. He said you would teach me." Pemblin heard the uncertainty in his own voice. "And show me something . . . I think." He shrugged his shoulders. "I don't know. I just don't think you should leave so quickly."

"Haven't I taught you something already?"

Pemblin thought. "Well, yes."

"Good," responded the spirit. "Then what remains is to show you, true?"

Pemblin pointed to himself. "Are you asking me?"

The spirit looked nervously around the room. He held up his stick defensively, like he was about to strike someone with it. "Who else is here that I should ask them?"

Pemblin was about to say his wife and children were sleeping, but he thought better of it. "No one else is here. And yes, you must show me the strength of Christmas Present."

The spirit lowered his defenses and examined Pemblin. "Indeed. I'll show you the might of Christmas Present." He pointed to a door that led to Pemblin's basement. "And so we go. Follow me, but watch out for the wolves," the spirit said with renewed vigor.

"Downstairs?"

"Are you to ask so many questions?" The spirit opened the door and descended the stairs to the basement.

Pemblin rolled his eyes and followed. When he reached the bottom of the stairs, he was no longer in his home. A man and a woman sat opposite each other at a dining table. The arrangement of food on their table was impressive, especially since there were only two of them. A large golden brown turkey, a great bowl of mashed potatoes with cheese sprinkled on top, a platter of sliced fruits and vegetables, fluffy rolls and other good foods.

The table was dressed in cloth the colors of cream and pumpkin, giving the room a distinct autumn feel. The décor reminded him of a leafy forest in the fall time. The lovely room had many windows, from which Pemblin could see a beautiful wilderness outside. Somehow it seemed familiar.

"Spirit?" Pemblin began.

"Quiet, Thomas G. Pemblin," the spirit scolded. "Let us watch and listen in peace."

"Well, Alvin, my dear. Should we?" On the surface, the woman looked very young, but behind her perfect makeup, Pemblin could see more of her true age. She was definitely beautiful, but past the prime years of her life. She put her fork down and extended her hand towards her companion, wiggling her fingers invitingly. Alvin, still chewing his food, nodded in agreement. He quickly swallowed and took her hand.

"I'll go first," she said.

"Alvin!" Pemblin exclaimed. "This is Alvin York. No

wonder the area looks familiar. He lives in my neighborhood, just down the street and around the corner."

"Yes," the spirit replied. "You have many neighbors. Few friends."

Pemblin frowned. That statement was an echo of his own observations. Hearing it from the spirit made it worse. It was hard for him to know for sure, but he suspected he was being chastized.

"In fact," the spirit continued, "he is more than just neighbor or friend to you." He ran a hand over his beard. "I dare say, Mr. Pemblin. It's my turn to ask a question. Do you recognize him?"

Pemblin smiled. "You *are* an absentminded spirit. Just like Scrooge said." Pemblin almost giggled. "I just told you who he was. That's Alvin York." Pemblin wanted to say that Alvin was his friend, but he didn't want to lie.

"Listen," the spirit entreated. He sounded annoyed with Pemblin.

"Please." Alvin smiled back at the woman. "Be my guest." He leaned back in the chair and placed his hands on his head.

"Hmm," she said. "Let me think. I'm thankful for my dearest Alvin, who, for a very short fifteen years, has been a faithful and devoted husband." She raised a glass in salute and drank.

"He sounds like a very nice fellow," Alvin said, a wry smile on his face. "I'll drink to him."

She winked affectionately. "Your turn."

"This won't be hard. I have lots to be thankful for." He held up his glass and smiled. "I'm thankful for the best wife, the best friend, the best housemate and. . ." he paused for unnecessary suspense, "the most beautiful woman I've ever laid eyes on."

She looked at him suspiciously. "Are you joking? This is supposed to be serious."

"I am serious," he defended. "Very serious."

She smiled, obviously pleased. "Okay. One more."

"Oh, really," he protested, slumping his shoulders. "That was all I got."

"Be quiet. It is Thanksgiving, after all."

Pemblin turned to the spirit, his forehead twisted in wavy wrinkles. "You *are* the Ghost of Christmas Present, right? She said it's Thanksgiving."

Pemblin feared he might get a whack from the spirit's stick. "Yes, yes," the spirit replied. "I *am* he. I am within my rights to show you this meeting." The spirit pointed to Alvin. "Do you know the man?"

Pemblin laughed. "Still absentminded. I told you I know the man as my *friend* and neighbor." He added friend this time.

"Know him from anywhere else?"

"I don't think so," Pemblin replied. "Should I?"

"I may be an absentminded spirit, but you're an absent-minded idiot," the spirit muttered.

The woman raised her glass. "I'm thankful for children." This last word evoked emotion from her, and she couldn't speak any more. The glass in her hand trembled. Her eyes filled with wetness and the room, though void of people, filled with the pungent scent of sadness.

Alvin looked on with moist eyes of his own. "Sylvia," he started.

She held up her hand like she wanted him to stop. She found her voice. "I may not be able to have them, but I'm thankful for them all the same." She smiled, a genuine but wet expression. "I'm thankful for children." She sipped from her glass.

Alvin took a drink from his glass and set it down on the table. "I'll drink to that, and say again, to my loving wife, the best and the most thankful person I've ever met." He looked at his watch. "Oops. I've gone and done it." He looked at Sylvia like he was reconsidering something. "I'll be late, but I don't want to leave you like this. Come with me," he invited. "Or do you want me to stay?"

"I'll be fine, Alvin." She waved him off. "But you should have taken today off. And your people too. They don't want to come in on a holiday."

"True. People *don't* want to work on holidays, but they want money." He moved to her side of the table and, taking her hand, knelt down. "I won't be long." He smiled at her and affectionately poked her leg with his finger. "Who would have thought the days from Thanksgiving to Christmas are the most profitable in all the year?" He kissed her on the cheek. "I'll be back in time to cuddle on the couch."

The spirit rested his heavy hand on Pemblin's shoulder. "There," he said as he pointed to a door in the dining room wall. "We go through there. Quickly now." His eyes darted over the room. "And watch out for wolves."

Pemblin entered the door and saw a conference room full

of people. Alvin sat at the head of a table and flipped through a stack of papers. He was engrossed in whatever information they gave him, but everyone else was deep in conversation.

The room was in the corner section of a building, and one half was made completely of windows. Outside, the setting sun filled the room with orange light. They were several stories off the ground, as Pemblin could see the backdrop of the city from where he stood. He was surprised when wolves appeared outside the window. They walked in the air, circling as if narrowing in on their prey.

"Spirit," Pemblin warned, "look at the wolves."

Christmas Present held his stick like a sword. "There are still only two. We have time yet."

"Okay, everyone." Alvin spoke above the chatter. He organized the papers into a neat stack. "Please have a seat." The room quieted, and Alvin became the focus of attention. While everyone else sat down, he stood and cleared his throat.

"Thank you for coming tonight. I know it's Thanksgiving, but I'll make it worth your time. We have one month to drive Christmas sales through the roof. This is nothing new, we do it every year. But I want to make sure we capitalize on the season as much as possible. We are going to hit our sales target, and you know what that means."

"A fat bonus!" a man shouted, to the cheers of his associates.

Alvin nodded. "Our task now is to overdrive so we blow our target out of the water and make that bonus something to remember. We have thirty minutes to come up with best in class ideas." He held his hands out invitingly. "You are the best minds this company has to offer." He nodded at a young woman who stood by a dry-erase board, pen in hand. "Alauna is going to write down our ideas. Shout them out."

People cleared their throats, wiped their noses, and coughed.

"Well," one person ventured, "I know that Zanigans is running a promotion on Christmas stockings. We could see if they'd be willing to partner with us. Buy one of their stockings and get a discount on our seasonal chocolate box."

"I like it," Alvin said. "Partnerships with other companies. Write that one down, Alauna." He turned back to the group. "What else?"

"Buy one get one free," someone yelled.

Alvin frowned. "I don't want to give stuff away." He looked contemplative. "But special promotions almost always result in a sales increase." He pointed to Alauna. "Write it down, please."

"I have an idea, but it may sound strange," a woman said. She looked apprehensive.

"You're amongst friends, Toni," Alvin encouraged. "Let's hear it."

"Yeah," the man next to her said. "We'll only judge you behind your back." The group laughed.

"Well," she said. "Does anything bother you about our Christmas banner?"

Alvin crinkled his chin. "The one that says 'Merry Christmas'?"

"That's it," she said. "That's the problem."

"Merry Christmas?"

"Not the merry part," she clarified. "The Christmas part."

Alvin's forehead wrinkled. "I'm not sure I'm following."

"The word 'Christmas' is holding us back. There are millions of people out there who aren't affiliated with Christmas. They don't identify with it. It's a religious word, isn't it?"

"I suppose it is. Why?"

"We spotlight the word 'Christmas' because we think it draws people to our product. What if it drives people away? What if Christmas offends some consumers? Is there a softer word that can capture both the Christmas crowd and the non-Christmas crowd?"

Alvin put a finger to his lips and paced. "Interesting. I think you're on to something." He pointed to Alauna. "Write it down. Remove the word 'Christmas' from our advertising campaign."

As Alauna wrote the strategy on the board, the window behind her filled with wolves. Pemblin counted them. "Spirit, there are five wolves outside."

"Yes," he confirmed. "Expect more before the night is over. There are wolves out there," he pointed to the windows, "and there are wolves in here." He waved his staff at the conference table. "I will be devoured."

"But they won't really remove the word 'Christmas,' will they?" Pemblin asked. "It's the Christmas season."

"I say again, I will be devoured." He pointed to the nearest door in the conference room. "Come, Mr. Pemblin. I will show you the *might* of Christmas Present. Through that door."

Pemblin ignored the conference room chatter, opened the door, and stepped inside.

He stood in a semi-familiar room. A piano was nestled against the wall, and musical instruments lay scattered throughout the room. Obviously some time had passed, but Pemblin definitely recognized the chorus director's room. There were bookcases with shelves full of file folders and disorganized papers, and a few coat hooks hung on the walls with instruments hanging from them. One wall held a multitude of picture frames.

"Recognize the man?" the Spirit asked, pointing to a photograph.

Pemblin examined the nearest photo. A choir of men and woman were organized in rows and columns in front of a church. On the front row and farthest to the right, was a short man dressed in a black tuxedo with a red bow tie around his neck.

"I remember the director and this wonderful choir. The Ghost of Christmas Past took me to see it again." Pemblin read the date stamped on the photo. "This picture was taken that night. It was the first performance of Handel's *Messiah* in my home town. I was just a child at the time." He breathed a heavy sigh. "Whoa. It's been forty years."

Pemblin scanned the other pictures. He read the labels and saw they were organized by year from left to right. The farther right the pictures went, the more recent the date. He read the year on the most recent picture. "Spirit, this was taken just last year. Has Dr. Leslie directed the *Messiah* every year?"

"Indeed, he has." The spirit spoke with gusto, obviously proud of the choir director. "People like him give me great strength."

The choir director stood in the same place in each photo, but with each passing year his hair became grayer, until in the most recent picture it was perfectly white. Year after year, the amount of people in the choir got smaller.

Pemblin looked around the room. There was dust on the instruments, and the books and papers looked abandoned. "Oh no," he sighed. "The director is dead, isn't he? And now that he's gone, there won't be a choir anymore." He shook his head. "Such a shame. Will they ever find a man like him to direct the music again?"

"He is not dead." The spirit pointed to the door. "He comes."

The director, with his flaming white hair, entered the room. He was old, but his eyes were bright, and his step had no less spring than that of decades earlier. He sat at the piano and began to play.

The music mesmerized Pemblin. With every chord, the musician channeled some special energy that made the notes more tangible and real. It was more than music; it was story. Christmas intertwined with sacrifice and perfection. This choir director had Christmas magic of his own.

Pemblin's mind was invaded by the sounds and scenes of Christmas. The joys and hopes, the sorrows and defeats, and at last the triumph. He glanced at the spirit and saw that even he, paranoid and ever fearful, was touched by the music.

The director stopped playing. He walked along the pictures and hummed. He paused when he got to the last one. "And who will sing now?" he said to the frame. He put on his coat and hat and opened the door to leave.

"Come," the spirit invited. "We must follow, but keep an eye out for the wolves. There are more of them now."

Pemblin didn't need to be coaxed. He wanted to see the choir again, no matter how small it was. "There it is, spirit." He pointed to the church. "That is where they sing." He beckoned for the spirit to walk faster. "Come, it will cheer you up."

Just then, he spotted the pack of wolves in the street, directly in their path. He counted eight, three more than the last time he'd seen them. Their chests were low to the ground and their hind legs cocked, like they were ready to pounce. They were dirty and gruesome.

Pemblin would have feared for himself, but the wolves never looked at him. He saw their eyes, their drooling fangs and their tight muscles, but it was clear they had no interest in him. They wanted the Ghost of Christmas Present, who at the moment looked very anxious.

"Spirit, what are these wolves which grow in number?"

"The most recent," he pointed to the largest in the pack, "the big one there." His fur coat was dark brown, almost black compared to the others. He stood at least a half foot higher than the rest. "That one is called Tradition. He is difficult to handle. He gave me this on my journey to you." He pointed to a gaping wound on his leg. "His sister, Falsehood, is close by. The rest of those dogs have no name but, answer to whatever ill description you give them."

"Why are they here now and not in Christmas's past? Scrooge never mentioned wolves."

The spirit, his stick poised like a sword, kept his eyes on the circling pack. "These wolves are older than Ebenezer Scrooge.

Older than the Ghost of Christmas Past, in fact. They've been hunting my kin since the beginning. They devour significance and meaning and leave behind emptiness."

"Look," Pemblin spotted the director. "He's passing the chapel. I thought he would go inside. We've got to catch up."

"Go," the Spirit commanded. "I can hold them off. They will still remember my staff. The wolves will not follow you."

Pemblin ran, and when he was close enough to touch the director, he slowed to a walk. He looked over his shoulder just in time to see the spirit knock a wolf to the ground with his staff.

One street beyond the church, they came to a school. They stopped in a large auditorium inside. The seats were full of teenagers. It was definitely a youthful group.

"It's good to see you, old friend." A man stepped forward to greet the director.

Dr. Leslie looked over the group. "This is what we have?"

The man nodded. "I'm sorry you haven't got enough support this year. How many have committed to sing?"

"Fifteen women and ten men. A quarter of what I need. I used to have so many that I didn't know what to do. The accompaniment we have is hardly a skeleton for a proper symphony." The director shrugged his shoulders and looked disappointed. "Everyone says they have no time."

"Getting commitments from people is hard for anyone these days," the man agreed. "You'd think it would be the opposite. We've so much technology that makes life easier. Why, I remember when I used to sit and do nothing but watch TV. It's strange how now that we have so many conveniences,

I have less time than ever. Ironic."

"I can't blame people for how they use their time." Dr. Leslie shrugged his shoulders. "But I wish I had more volunteers."

"Well," the man said, "let's see what younger, less complicated lives can contribute." He leaned his head toward the bleachers. "These are my students. Invite them all."

"Thanks, William." He patted his friend on the shoulder. "Here goes."

The director faced the students and projected his voice. "It's fitting that an old man like me should ask young people for help. The youth of the world are the future of it, right? And we have something in common, you and I." He scanned the faces, wincing, like he wasn't sure that was something he wanted to admit. "After all, our talents in music are among the services we provide to the poor in spirit. And the season of help is upon us." He smiled his most charming smile.

"I have a small choir that performs on Christmas Eve night. I don't have enough bodies to do the music justice. There are plenty of singers good enough, but most are busy. Therefore, I invite all of you to come and sing in my choir." He pointed to a few instruments on the ground. "I especially need musicians who can play the trumpet, the violin, and the bass.

"I would be very grateful if you would join us. However, as the music we perform has a special purpose, I hope you would dedicate the time necessary to make it perfect."

"Um, like how much time?" a girl spoke, lifting her eyes from her cell phone.

The director smiled at her. "Like, a few hours a night until the performance. Mr. Turnbough has agreed to give you extra credit if you participate. But I think the experience should be reward enough."

"Sorry," a young man said as he put his backpack on. "I'd love to help, but I have to work in the evenings after school. I can't take the time off." He got up, and a few others shouted that they, too, had to work.

"Sorry, pops. It's basketball season, and I can't miss practice," the tallest said as he excused himself. More followed and as they walked by, each gave a reason why they couldn't sing. "Wrestling," one said. "Volleyball," another said. "Cross-country," a few more said. "I don't want to," one said.

The director counted those left. "Eleven." He smiled at the remaining. "We start tonight. Please come to the North-folk chapel at six p.m. If you know anyone else who can participate, please invite them. Brothers and sisters, moms and dads. Anybody."

The gym cleared, and the director put his arm around his friend. "Thanks again. Will they show up?"

"We can hope, right? We can hope."

The door to the auditorium crashed open, and the Ghost of Christmas Present entered. He took several steps, supporting himself with his staff, and then fell to his knees. He had fresh cuts on his arms and legs and across his chest. Blood dripped to the floor beneath him.

Pemblin ran to his side and propped him against the near-est wall. He supported the spirit's head with his hand and wiped at the blood with his sleeve. Pemblin looked at his impromptu handkerchief after he'd swiped at the blood. It was perfectly clean. He tried to sop up the blood again but could not.

"Spirit, I'm not sure how to help you. What can I do?"

"You may yet be of use to me. Take me to that door." He pointed across the auditorium.

There could not have been a door that was farther away, and Pemblin didn't think the spirit could walk that far. "Spirit, can we go through this door?" He nodded at the closest one. "It's not as far a walk. Use your Christmas magic and take us through this door. We need to get you somewhere safe."

The spirit shook his head and swallowed hard. He looked thirsty. His face dripped sweat, and smears of dirt ran across his cheeks.

"Can I get you something to drink?" Pemblin's concern was evident. "Where's your magic cup that's never empty? I'll get it for you."

"Not the door behind us." The spirit struggled to speak. "That is the door we came through. It got us to where we are. We mustn't go back that way." He pointed to the far door. "Thomas G. Pemblin, that door, if you please."

"Spirit, I don't think that's a good idea. You're in no condition to go anywhere."

"Take courage, Pemblin. I am not flesh and blood. These wounds are given to me by people like you. The least you can do is help me to that door."

Pemblin was in shock. He didn't know what to say. He was angry, then sad, then angry again. "I gave you these wounds? People like me? I love Christmas. I would never hurt you."

"No." The spirit shook his head. "You love something, but

it isn't me. You can't love something you don't know."

"The wolves did this to you," Pemblin defended. "I saw you fight them." He put his hands on his hips and tried not to shout. "You can't think straight like this. You're delirious," he accused. His face burned hot.

The spirit writhed in agony. "The door, Pemblin. Take me to the door!"

Pemblin heard a low growl from the other side of the wall. He acted quickly. He hoisted the spirit and rested him over his shoulders. "No offense, but I hope our journey together is over. You're not as enjoyable as I'd hoped."

The spirit managed a hopeless smile. "Who is having the worse time, you or I?" He winced as he limped.

"Easy," Pemblin said as he steadied him. "You did fight off the wolves, didn't you?"

"I bought us time. The worst is nearby. Fear her."

"Falsehood?"

"Yes. She is the master of the pack. Her teeth are small, but sharp. They cut into your flesh without you knowing it."

Pemblin opened the door. "Oh, good," he breathed. "We're home. Look, Spirit, it's my living room. You're safe now." He helped the spirit through the doorway.

"I'm not sure why you think that," the spirit muttered. "Nowhere is safe."

Pemblin ignored him. "There's a grand old Christmas tree for you. And plenty of packages for the little ones when they wake up. It will be a wonderful Christmas."

"And so you say," the spirit replied. "You don't mind if I sit, do you?"

"Not at all." Pemblin was so happy to be home and around his own version of Christmas that he could have skipped through the room. "I'll go get us something to drink. Something to lighten the load."

He'd taken a few steps when he heard whispering. He stopped and looked at the Spirit, a finger to his lips. "Shhh." The spirit did it back, letting Pemblin know he understood. The sound of footsteps on the stairs told him someone was coming. He hid himself just as Jillian and Lisa tiptoed into the room.

"Wow," Lisa exclaimed. She pointed to the gifts. "Santa came." She clasped her hands and started to bounce like a spring.

"Check the cookies," Jillian said. "If they're gone, we'll know he *really* came." They ran to the plate they'd thoughtfully left by the tree.

Jillian gasped. "Look, they're gone. He is so real."

"Yep, I knew it." Lisa wrapped her arms around her chest like she was giving herself a hug. "He's real."

Pemblin beamed, proud he'd eaten the cookies.

"Wait," Lisa said. "What about the reindeer food?" Her eyebrows lifted in concern. They ran to the front door. Lisa picked up the empty bowl and held it for Jillian to see. "Empty," she sang.

"Amazing." Jillian's nose crinkled when she smiled.

"Thomas G. Pemblin," the spirit whispered.

"Shhh," Pemblin hushed.

"I can't remember why we are quiet. Is it to hide from the wolves, or from your children?"

"I don't want the girls to hear us," Pemblin whispered. He paused as realization came to him. "What wolves? There are no wolves in my house."

"You have forgotten your senses, Mr. Pemblin. Your children can't see us. I am still your guide." He closed his eyes. "For now." The spirit spoke slowly, clearly exhausted. "They can't see you or me, remember, my absentminded friend. There is no need to be quiet. Come now, Mr. Pemblin. Observe the majesty of Christmas Present in your own home."

In the window, the sun began to rise, and the spirit pointed to the living room entryway. Mr. Pemblin watched himself walk into the room. His mirror image yawned and scratched his stomach. The real Pemblin rubbed his own stomach, confused as to who was touching his belly, his shadow or himself.

"Merry Christmas," said Pemblin's shadow.

Jillian and Lisa looked at him. "Daddy," they screamed. They hugged his legs.

Both Pemblins smiled, but only the shadow spoke. "So, did Santa bring you anything?"

"He came, Daddy," Lisa exclaimed. "He really came. He ate the cookies and he left us presents."

"It's true," Jillian confirmed. "And the reindeer ate their food."

"Wow," the shadow said. "I guess he is real." He bent down and kissed them both on the head.

Mrs. Pemblin walked into the room. "Merry Christmas, sweethearts!" She scanned the room. "Where's Gordi?"

"I'm here." He came in behind her. His head was down,

hung over his phone, the birthday present from the night before. He slid his finger across the screen. "Wow," he said as he looked at the tree. "That's a lot of presents."

"And stockings, too," Jillian added excitedly. "You can't forget the stockings."

"Gordi!" Lisa exclaimed. "Santa came. See!" She pointed to the new packages under the tree and held up the empty cookie plate.

"You guys must have been really good this year," Mrs. Pemblin said. She spied Gordi as he slid his finger across his phone again. "Gordi, I said put that away."

He groaned and slipped the phone in his pocket. He slumped in the chair next to the Ghost of Christmas Present. The real Pemblin sat down on the other side of Gordi, miffed that he wasn't really in the room with his family.

The morning unfurled just like Pemblin thought it should. Unwrapped package after unwrapped package, and thank you after thank you, until all was finished. Pemblin's shadow gathered his family around him.

"Look, spirit," Pemblin said excitedly. "This is one of my favorite parts."

"Gordi, Jillian, and Lisa," the shadow said, looking at their bright and happy faces, "what a wonderful morning it's been. I want you to write a thank you letter to each person who gave you a gift. Tell them thank you for what they gave you and wish them merry Christmas."

"Even Santa?" asked Jillian.

"Especially Santa," the shadow said as he touched her nose.

Jillian and Lisa scurried away to write their notes, but

Gordi stayed on the couch. "Do I really have to write a letter to Santa?" He looked at his father discouragingly. "I know he isn't real," Gordi whispered.

The shadow looked stern. "Did Santa bring you a gift?"

"Come on, Dad," he protested. "He's not real."

"So what if he's not, we need to show gratitude. What better way to show you're grateful than by writing a thank-you note?"

The shadows of Pemblin and his family evaporated. "See, spirit. There are still those who honor Christmas." He tapped the spirit's hand gently. "That should heal your wounds."

The spirit laughed amidst labored breathing. "You think you've done Christmas a service here." He lifted his finger and pointed to the tree. "That is not what I witnessed. Thomas G. Pemblin, is there no better way to show appreciation for the sacred day that is Christmas than by writing a letter to Santa?"

Pemblin was abashed. He stuttered over his words. "I just want everyone to be thankful and remember where their gifts come from. I don't write a letter to Santa. It's for the children."

The spirit coughed and choked. "And where is true Christmas celebrated?"

Pemblin paused, searching for the right answer. "I keep the meaning of Christmas in my heart."

"And so you don't keep it at all. Listen here, Thomas G. Pemblin, and listen well. Santa is not real."

Pemblin was insulted. "I know."

"Then why have your little ones pay homage to that which cannot give them lasting fulfillment? To teach them to have faith in something that is not real is mockery of that which is real." The spirit laughed. "Write a letter to Santa." His laughter turned to coughing. "Should you not also teach them to give thanks to He who is the author of the season, to He who owns Christmas day?" The spirit's eyes opened wide. "You, Pemblin, have let loose the wolf named Falsehood!" He pointed behind Pemblin.

A ghastly creature stood in the window. It looked like two wolves combined into one. Four eyes on a large misshapen head, four legs, and two tails. Its black breath fogged the window. As he looked on Falsehood, Pemblin began to tremble. He locked eyes with the creature.

"Spirit," he said as he rose, keeping an eye on the wolf, "thank you for what you've shown me, but I'd like our time to end. I'm ready for my third visitor now."

"It cannot be, Mr. Pemblin. One more thing to see." He pointed to the closet door. "That door." His voice was raggedy and shallow.

"But Spirit," Pemblin pleaded, "You must leave before you are killed. You should have moved on by now. Right?"

"I am the weakest of all spirits, Mr. Pemblin. Shouldn't you harken to me like a physician harkens to the sick?"

Pemblin shook his head. "But what can I do to make you whole? I'm not a doctor."

"Take me to the door before we *both* are devoured. Yes, Pemblin." The spirit coughed and pointed at Falsehood. "She can see you. She is different than other wolves. Not a wolf at all. Not a creature at all!" Christmas Present tried to get up, but slumped down. "To the door!" he yelled.

Pemblin helped him off the ground. He looked at the window to keep tabs on Falsehood, but she had disappeared.

They made it to the door. Pemblin pushed it open and stepped inside.

With the spirit draped over his shoulder, Pemblin took in his surroundings. He was playing part in a demonic horror story. They stood at the end of a long and narrow hallway with doors down both sides. It looked like a hospital wing.

"Spirit," Pemblin asked, "why are we here?"

Christmas Present licked his lips, a dry cracking sound, like two stones knocking together. "It's Christmas here too, you know. Christmas morning. . . ." His head dropped.

"Spirit!" Pemblin shook the limp body on his shoulder. "Spirit!"

Christmas Present opened his eyes. "I'm here, Thomas. We haven't much time. Walk. Look into the doors." The spirit winced.

Pemblin stepped forward and looked in the first door. To his relief, it was empty. Inside there was a small nightstand and dresser next to a simple bed with a metal frame. "There's nothing inside," he said.

The spirit pointed forward.

Cautiously, Pemblin moved to the next door and slowly looked inside. An old man lay in bed. He wasn't moving, just lying with his eyes open, staring at the ceiling. The room was mostly bare, furnished exactly like the previous one. The only difference Pemblin could see was a picture frame on the nightstand. It was difficult to tell if the man was one of the images in the picture. He was so old and emaciated that the happy smiling people in the photo seemed hundreds of years away.

"Who is he?" Pemblin asked.

"He is Loneliness. There are many who answer to that name." The spirit swallowed hard. A painful and forced sound echoed from his throat. "The next door, please."

Pemblin walked to the next door and leaned against the frame, not committed to going inside. A woman lay in the bed. Like the man in the room next to her, she looked very old, but was more alert. She roused herself from bed and walked very slowly across the room, taking short and choppy steps. She reached a rocking chair and carefully sat down.

Her room was decorated with the same simple furnishings, but there were more picture frames scattered about. Some of the photos were recent. Pemblin could tell because the woman in the photos wasn't any younger than the real person he was looking at. She was surrounded by smiling people. Next to her chair was an end table with a short stack of letters in a neat pile. The edges of the envelopes were smudged with finger prints, evidence of repeated use. With lethargic and clumsy fingers, she opened an envelope and took out a letter. Her glossy eyes moved over the page. A tired smile slid across her face.

"Spirit," Pemblin asked, "is she also called Loneliness?"

His voice was breathy, mostly air without sound. "She is Longing."

"Longing?" Pemblin repeated.

"Yes. She wants. Interaction, friendship and human touch."

"I see the people in the pictures. They look happy with her. The pictures are recent, too."

"Indeed," the spirit whispered. "Next door."

Pemblin's will to go farther wavered. He didn't want to be in this place. He contemplated an exit strategy. Truly, the spirit could not make good decisions. He should help the spirit where the spirit could not help himself. They needed a safe place, away from Falshood, Tradition, and the other wolves.

But what to do? Could he open any door and be transported away? He wanted to be home again, not some distant place, a memory or future. Home. In his bed on Christmas Eve with his wife. Home.

Christmas Present shakily raised his head, his eyes level with Pemblin's. Their faces were uncomfortably close. Pemblin wanted to look away, but before he did, the spirit whispered.

"I am devoured." The Spirit was ripped away from Pemblin.

The hallway was full of wolves. Trapped in the jaws of Falsehood was the bare foot of Christmas Present, who struggled hopelessly to escape.

Pemblin reached for the spirit's outstretched arm, but Falsehood leapt down the hallway, leading the pack of wolves and the spirit out of reach. With each passing room, the spirit tried to grab the door post, but his effort was useless. The spirit screamed as he scraped along the floor, leaving a smear of blood on the sterile tile.

He chased after them, but it was useless. In every door he passed, he saw more people in their beds. They called to him as he ran, pleading for his attention. The more he ignored them, the louder their cries became. He covered his ears with his hands and continued to run.

At the end of the hallway he came to a closed door. The trail of blood continued under it, one solid line of red liquid. Pemblin fought back fear and the sudden urge to cry. He pushed the door open and stepped inside.

THE GHOST OF
CHRISTMAS YET TO COME

Pemblin stood in his bedroom. His chest heaved in and out like he'd just run a marathon. His wife was still sleeping on her side of the bed. Outside it continued to snow. It was Christmas, but Pemblin had no joy in his heart. He felt no excitement about the day to come.

He couldn't erase the image of Christmas Present reaching for help. Echoes of the spirit's screams reverberated in his ears. Pemblin could do nothing but watch the wolves carry the spirit away. His knees began to tremble, and in an unexpected harrumph, he collapsed on the floor. He wanted to wake up from this nightmare.

He loved the Christmas season. Or at least he thought he did. Or was it that he loved *his* Christmas? His version. He was confused. There was no place to catalog his feelings and thoughts, so they floated around and smashed into each other, causing explosions in his brain. He wished he could slip into oblivion, where thought and feeling couldn't attack him.

But it wasn't to be so.

Gray mist appeared on the floor, spreading like ocean

waves on the sand. Dozens of smoky tendrils swirled around him and filled the room. The fog billowed from underneath his door. It came from outside the bedroom.

It was happening. His third and final visitation. Ebenezer Scrooge had told him to expect three visitors. He'd enjoyed the Spirit of Christmas Past, but abhorred his time with the Spirit of Christmas Present. If the night's pattern were to continue, his next visitor would be the Spirit of Christmas Yet to Come. In the case of Ebenezer Scrooge, this was the spirit that should be feared above all others.

As it was, Pemblin was done with visitors. He wished he could wake up and celebrate Christmas as he saw fit. He wasn't ready for the Ghost of Christmas Future.

His wishes didn't matter.

"Thomas G. Pemblin," a familiar voice called. 'Twas the same voice he'd heard on the wind as he entered his home that day. "Come here," the voice demanded.

He wanted to disobey. But he found himself walking toward the door.

His entire house was filled with the fog. It slid along the walls, along the floor, and wound itself around the banister. When he walked down the stairs, it puffed around his feet and legs like tiny, wicked hands.

The Ghost of Christmas Yet to come.

His thoughts should be happy, for Christmases yet to be lived would be full of joy. Yet, as he descended the stairs, he wondered if he, like Ebenezer Scrooge, was destined for the dark figure in long robes whose hands were bones without flesh. Could the Ghost of Christmas Future truly be the Grim Reaper?

Pemblin reached the entryway to his living room. It was there he had his Christmas tree. It was there he had stockings and wrapped gifts. It was there he and his family would sit on the morrow and enjoy Christmas day. It should be a happy place to enter, but he didn't feel happy, only trepidation. He watched the fog waft by. He waited.

"Enter," the voice commanded.

Pemblin closed his eyes and forced himself to be calm. "Christmas magic," he whispered. "Christmas magic." He turned the corner and stepped into the room.

"Scrooge?" Ebenezer Scrooge stood in the center of the room. He was still dressed in his nineteenth-century suit, the same ornate top hat on his head.

"I am he." Scrooge grabbed the brim of his hat and pulled it down like he was taking a bow.

Pemblin searched the room, thinking there must be someone else. There was no one. "Ebenezer, are you the Ghost of Christmas Future?"

"I am not."

Pemblin relaxed. "Honestly, I'm relieved. I've had enough of spirits." He smiled tiredly at Ebenezer. "Present company excluded. Was the Ghost of Christmas Future supposed to come?"

"Indeed he was." Scrooge removed the hat from his head. "You may yet know him before the night is over."

"Oh." Pemblin heard the disappointment in his own voice. "Then the night isn't over." He felt like he'd been awake for days. He didn't want to say it out right, but Christmas was ruined. The sooner the night ended, the sooner he would rest. An ironic twist of time.

Scrooge shook his head. "Not over indeed." He smiled playfully. "I shall be your guide on that which is to come. Mind you, Pemblin, I am not a spirit like those you've seen tonight. I don't possess the magic they do. But my heart is full of Christmas joy, and therefore I have some magic. There are few who love this season like I do. Few were changed by it like I was." He tapped his finger against his nose. "I hope your heart will be moved like mine was so long ago."

Pemblin cringed. There it was again. He, a man who had lived each day with Christmas in his heart, a man who strove to honor the season, needed a change of heart.

"Ebenezer." Pemblin's pride was inflamed. "Do I really need to change that much? Before your repentance, you where the chiefest of misers. Is my life so unworthy that I *need* a change of heart?"

Scrooge's eyes moistened. "No, you are not as great a sinner as I. And yes, you need a change of heart so you may bear that which lies ahead." Scrooge removed his hat. "Here, Thomas. Take my hat. Place it on your head and you shall see what I see."

Pemblin took it and exhaled. "This night has truly been unforgettable."

"Filled with Christmas magic," Scrooge added with a wink. "Place it on your head."

The moment the hat touched his head, they were no longer in Pemblin's living room. They stood in the familiar chorister's office. He wasn't sure if it was the frequent visits or the man's unparalleled quest for musical perfection, but Pemblin had grown very fond of the old choir director.

Pemblin noticed the fog had followed them. Just like in his home, the wispy tendrils grew over the walls like vines in a jungle. "Ebenezer," Pemblin asked, "why is that smoke following us? It's a little ominous, don't you think? Is it a sign that the Ghost of Christmas Yet to Come is nearby?"

"Take courage, Mr. Pemblin," Scrooge comforted. "The future is not yet solidified. We look through the fog of that which is to come. It will follow us tonight. And the Ghost of Christmas Yet to Come, you may yet know him before the night is over."

"That's what I'm afraid of," Pemblin mumbled.

Dr. Leslie was undeniably old. His head and shoulders had fought gravity for so long that they drooped low. He sat at his piano bench playing a melody until he was interrupted by knocking at his door.

Slowly, he got off the bench and opened the door. "Good evening," he greeted, his voice shaky but bright. "Please come in. Come in."

Two men dressed in business suits entered the room. "Good evening to you, too, Dr. Leslie," one of them said. "I have to tell you, I'm a big fan of your work. I've attended your Christmas Eve performance as often as I could. It's a favorite Christmas tradition in my home."

Dr. Leslie nodded. "Thank you. I'm sure this year's concert is the last one I will ever conduct. I doubt there's enough life in me to make it another year. But don't worry, gentleman, I've got a list of potential directors to take my place." He shuffled back to the piano and grabbed a sheet of paper. He held it out for them to take. "Here are my recommendations."

"Thank you, but that won't be necessary," the second man said. "That's why we've come to see you tonight. Unfortunately, there will be no more Christmas Eve concerts. Not this year, and probably not in the years to come. Not for a while, anyway."

Dr. Leslie looked confused, like the man had spoken a foreign language. "What do you mean there won't be any more? We've been doing it for almost fifty years. I know participation fluctuates, but we get by with help from the school board. They give extra credit to kids who sing in the Christmas choir."

The man put up his hands defensively, more dramatic than was necessary. "Like I said, I'm a big fan of your devotion to the music. But, well, support is lacking, and people just aren't coming like they used to. Last year there were hardly a hundred people who listened to the performance." The man leaned up on his toes and then rocked back on his heels. "People aren't buying tickets, and we think the space could be used more wisely."

"More profitably, you mean." The director looked like he'd sucked on a lemon. "I still don't know why you started charging people for the concert. Anyway, I don't care how many people listen." Dr. Leslie pointed his finger at the man, like he was blaming him for something. "It's not just for them, you know. People seen and unseen listen to the music."

The two men exchanged looks. "The church committee has decided to change the program. We want to give people a rest from the ancient ballads."

"Give people a rest?" The director looked like he'd been slapped in the face. "Rest from what?"

"We'd like to liven it up a bit, put on a show more suitable for children and attract a younger crowd. We're going to make a great big event out of Christmas Eve. There will be snowmen and reindeer," the man winked, "and you-know-who will be there."

"The Messiah?" Dr. Leslie asked accusingly. "Will he be there?" The edge in his voice made him sound more vivacious than a typical eighty-year-old.

"Oh, of course, that too," the man added. "There will be a nativity and barn animals for the children to pet."

"And we'd like you to come," the other man chimed in, eager to make the director happy. "You've quite the reputation, and we think it would set the right tone if people saw you leading a stirring rendition of 'Here Comes Santa Claus.' We'll all sing it when the big man shows up."

The director stared at them.

"Well," one of them asked, "will you?"

"I wish I'd died yesterday," he said. "No, I will not direct a stirring rendition of 'Here Comes Santa Claus.' I'm sure there's no such thing. Now if you'll excuse me." He put on his coat and hat and left the men standing in his office.

Pemblin and Scrooge followed the director as he walked with hands in his pockets. Pemblin wondered if there was a point to following him, as Dr. Leslie clearly had no choir to conduct. Their path took them to a local shopping center. He walked down an aisle of the store, his head low. He paid no attention to the hustle and bustle of shoppers around him. He didn't look at any product on the shelf, or at any of the advertising or great deals. It seemed to Pemblin that the old man was oblivious to everything.

They walked to the music department, and the director stopped. He ran his finger across the titles and tracks of the holiday music. He read them aloud.

"'Frosty the Snow man,' 'Jingle Bell Rock,' 'Rudolph the Red-Nosed Reindeer,' 'Jolly Old Saint Nicolas,' 'I want a Hippopotamus for Christmas'. . . ." his voice trailed off, but he continued to run his hand along the music until he'd read every title.

"No 'Silent Night'. No 'Angels from on High'. No Christmas." A tear fell down his wrinkly face.

"Excuse me," a store employee said. "Are you okay?"

The old man put his hands over his ears. "I can't stand this music."

The young man grimaced. "Is that why you're crying?"

"Oh, never mind," the old man dismissed.

"I love this song," the employee said. "Everybody does."

"If I hear 'Jingle Bell Rock' one more time, I'm going to have a heart attack." The old man turned and walked away. "Gone." He shook his head. "It's all gone."

Pemblin watched the director walk away, and the smoky vines grew until they encompassed everything. The music and the store disappeared, and he stood with Scrooge in the clouds. They walked in the mist, nothing below or in front of them.

"Once, a young man stood on the doorstep of my clerk's

office," Scrooge said. As he walked he kicked up puffs of fog. "He sang to me a Christmas song. It was a story of a man who traversed a deadly storm so he could provide food and comfort to the poor." Scrooge hummed a few notes. "That was a good Christmas song. One you don't hear much." He continued to hum.

"I don't recognize that tune, Scrooge," Pemblin said. "Is it a Christmas carol?"

"Good King Wenceslas." Scrooge hummed some more. "That is what it's called."

The clouds receded, revealing the ornate conference room that Pemblin had seen with the Ghost of Christmas Present. He recognized Alvin immediately. People danced to lively music; there were plates of food and bouts of laughter. A multitude of congratulations and clasping hands, hugs and opened bottles of wine.

Alvin stood at the head of the conference table; his hands raised high as he shouted. "Congratulations!" He pounded the desk for emphasis. "Never before has this company seen growth like this." He whistled. "Toni," he pointed at a woman. "Excellent strategy. A bit nontraditional, if you know what I mean." He laughed. "Really. Who would have thought removing Christmas from Christmas would expand our sales footprint? I had no idea the season was so divisive." He raised his glass. "To you!"

She smiled bashfully, obviously loving the attention.

A bald man with a fat belly climbed on the table and beat his chest like a gorilla. "Henceforth," he shouted, "there shall be no more Christmas. Only Happy Holidays and Season's

Greetings. And profits through the roof!"

"Here, here," they cheered.

"Get off the table, Jared." Alvin pointed to the floor. "Now, please. The last thing I need is a workman's comp claim."

"Ebenezer," Pemblin asked. "They're joking, right?"

"Humbug. Indeed they are not." Scrooge pointed to a man who sat alone in the corner of the conference room. He looked like he could be the oldest in the group; his hair was mostly gone and his forehead was a permanent valley of wrinkles. His eyebrows were thick as weeds and his ears looked too large for his balding head. "There are others who recognize the loss. Watch that man there. His name is Benjamin. He is many things to Alvin, but mostly a trusted advisor and uncle."

Alvin drank the last of his wine, and it spilled over his cheeks. "I'm going home," he declared, "to share the spoils of the season with my wife." He slipped into his overcoat. "Everyone can do as they wish."

He got a few steps down the hallway and someone yelled his name. He turned around. "Uncle Ben!" Alvin put his arm around Ben's shoulder and walked with him.

"Merry Christmas, Uncle. Could you believe it? I'd never imagined us as sculptors of society. We mold this nation with our strategy." He raised his fist in the air and shook it dramatically. "We determine what the masses buy and what they celebrate. We determine the food that goes on their table and when they put it there. I'm half-tempted to remove the Easter Bunny from Easter and in his place put a fish, just to prove that we can. Such power." He chuckled heartily. "Merry Christmas."

"Merry today, maybe." The old man's voice was deep, and his tone calculated. "But maybe not tomorrow."

Alvin stopped and looked at his uncle. "Something's bothering you. What is it? And don't try and hide it. I can tell when something's got you."

"Well," he said, "I won't be afraid to speak my mind, then. I couldn't be prouder of the man you've become." He smiled and took Alvin's hand. "Your father built this company from the ground up. He was such a good man, and I remember how he struggled for the longest time to make this work. But he kept with it and made something happen. He changed all our lives. He would be so proud of you. I miss my brother, and at times I look at you and see him."

Alvin looked at him skeptically. "But?"

Ben shrugged his shoulders. "But, I can't say that back there was your best moment. Or best for your father's legacy."

Alvin's countenance dimmed. "I'm listening."

"I like all days that I'm not dead, but Christmas happens to be one of my favorites. You might have just put a dagger in the heart of what so many hold sacred." Ben hesitated. "And for money. Something you have plenty of."

"Oh, Uncle," Alvin said. "I meant no harm, and neither do they." He pointed to the conference room. "We are happy to have good returns on our time."

"Do you remember what your father used to do this time of year? He was more concerned about putting a few good things in other people's pockets than in his own. He loved you and all his children, and I know he made you happy during this season, but it was Christmas that brought the excitement.

Not holiday or season's greetings, though those were part of it. And I wouldn't take them away. But it was Christmas. Always Christmas and his children in December."

"He could do that, Uncle. He *had* children." Alvin's tone betrayed a hidden wound. "What is Christmas without children?"

Uncle Ben smiled compassionately, and his eyes filled with tears. "Alvi, my boy. They are all your children. Every single one of them."

Pemblin perked. "Alvi? The little boy and his father that I saw at the run-down apartments?" He turned to Ebenezer. "The boy Alvi is Alvin York, my neighbor?" Pemblin chided himself for not making the connection sooner.

Scrooge nodded. "The very same."

"What a remarkable transformation his father must have gone through. To be so poor and then to have built this." Pemblin pointed to the walls around him. "He sounds like an incredible man."

"He was," Scrooge agreed. "Alvin would do well to follow his father's example."

Pemblin was troubled. He put his hand over his mouth and let his thoughts materialize.

"Ebenezer, Alvin may deserve censorship for removing Christmas from his business campaign, but he didn't destroy Christmas. Not for those who really keep it. He made commodities available to the masses. Why can't people buy and receive gifts and show generosity during the Christmas season? These are not evil things. Is anything wrong with Frosty the Snowman or Rudolph the Red-Nosed Reindeer, or too many presents under the tree?"

Scrooge eyed Pemblin thoughtfully. "I don't think there is anything wrong with these things," he said. "After all, I'm a ghost filled with Christmas magic. If I can stand before you, then why can't Frosty and reindeer and Santa be a part of the Christmas magic too?"

"Then what should we do?" Pemblin inquired. "Can we not celebrate Christmas and keep it too?"

"Well said, Mr. Pemblin," Scrooge agreed. "Celebrate Christmas and keep it too. Make and be merry, for yourself, your family and friends. Yet remember, by aiding those around you who have not, you honor Christmas. Pemblin, my dear fellow, do you know the needs of those within your influence?"

Pemblin thought of his wife and children, but then he thought of Brian Hartwick, his neighbor. He thought of the Yorks, and his colleagues at work. He thought of his sister, whom he'd hardly spoken to in a year, and his mom and dad. Weren't they all in his influence? Pemblin didn't know any of their needs.

Know the needs of those within your influence? The question reminded him of his wife's admonition before she went to sleep. "I will hold you responsible," she'd said. Pemblin wasn't sure how or why, but he connected the two thoughts, like they were one and the same. His heart began to ache.

Scrooge made a sour face. "Destroy celebration? Humbug to that. I'll take no part of it." He put a finger to his nose. "But let not celebration overpower that which is celebrated. And let not that which is imaginary diminish that which is both sacred and real."

The fog eclipsed everything, swallowing Alvin and his uncle. When it receded again, Pemblin stood with Scrooge in a concrete driveway, which was connected to a large and beautiful house. The windows were vast and ornately shaped, the front door twice the size of a man, and the roof arched in several places like a gothic cathedral. Giant trees circled the gate and yard, making it feel like they were in a forest.

"This is a beautiful home," Pemblin said.

"A beautiful building, yes," Scrooge said. "Don't be so quick to call it a home. You don't know what transpires inside."

"Who lives here?"

"Come. I'll show you."

They walked down the driveway until they reached the street, and Pemblin saw the neighborhood. Each home was grand and beautiful in its own way. Houses like these were not meant for normal people. Only the extravagantly wealthy could afford them. Pemblin considered himself a wealthy man, having built his own success from counseling others in their finances. As successful as he was, and as much money as he had, he knew he could never sustain a life in the smallest of these houses.

"This is a beautiful neighborhood," he remarked, looking at Scrooge to see what commentary he would add. Pemblin expected to be contradicted.

"Indeed, Mr. Pemblin. A beautiful neighborhood."

An engine revved, and a bright red sports car appeared on the road. It moved quickly down the street, wheels screeching on the pavement. It swerved into the driveway, almost hitting the brick mailbox next to Ebenezer and Pemblin. The license plate had eight bold letters: ENTITLED.

"That's a strange thing to put on your car," Pemblin said. He looked at Scrooge and joked, "I dislike the driver already."

Scrooge put his hand on the mailbox and nodded for Pemblin to read the name inscribed on it.

"Gordon Pemblin?" Pemblin raised his eyebrows. "Gordi?" He looked at Scrooge disbelievingly. "It can't be." Before Ebenezer answered, Pemblin began running after the car.

"Humbug to running, Mr. Pemblin," Scrooge shouted. "I haven't done it in centuries."

A tall and slender man got out of the car. His head was covered with perfectly groomed brown hair. His skin was tanned and the muscles in his forearms were tight. In Pemblin's opinion, he was handsome.

"Gordi!" Pemblin yelled.

"He can't hear you, Mr. Pemblin," Scrooge reminded, panting as he rested his hands on his knees. "Christmas magic, remember."

Gordon's pocket began to sing. He pulled out a phone and answered it. "Lisa," he shouted into the receiver. "How's my favorite little sister? Are you coming over? It's my birthday." Gordon laughed. "Fantastic. And then you must stay for tomorrow. It's Christmas, and it will be a party you won't forget." He nodded his head like he was agreeing to something she said. "Great," he answered. "We'll count on it. No, don't bring anything. There is tons of food here. It's all catered by Glenda Morize. I'm sure you've heard of her. She only does the most upscale events," he boasted. "She costs a lot, but she's worth it. We'll see you soon."

Pemblin was proud. "See, Ebenezer," he said, his smile wide and beaming, "there are still people who honor Christmas and keep it right."

Gordon's phone rang again. He read the name on the screen and bit his lip. "On Christmas Eve?" He put the phone back in his pocket and walked in the front door. "I'm not answering that one," he mumbled.

Pemblin had been struck by the grandeur of the house while he stood outside of it. But now that he stood inside, he wasn't impressed. It was bare, almost hollow, like there wasn't enough of anything to justify the space. There were a few pictures on the walls, but they didn't belong. Economy frames displaying generic mountains and rivers, a few portraits of the stars, but nothing that fit the arched doorways and temple-like walls.

He looked for pictures of family, but saw none. The walls were massive, but their bareness made them seem stale and cold. A giant chandelier hung in the entryway, but it gave no light when Gordon flipped the switch. The only light streamed in through the windows.

Gordi flipped the switch up and down and looked at the chandelier, like he was expecting it to do something. "Margret!" The veins on his neck bulged.

Pemblin flinched and turned to Scrooge. "Who's Margret?"

"Your daughter-in-law. A very promising young woman when she married your son."

"Well, of course she is," Pemblin agreed. "I'd expect

nothing less for Gordi. He was always the best child."

"I said *was*, Pemblin," Ebenezer corrected. "She *was* a promising young woman. And then she married Gordon."

A thin but pretty woman walked into the foyer. In one hand she had a large steak knife and in the other she held a full glass of wine. Her head wobbled back and forth as she stood with her feet wide apart, like she was having trouble keeping her balance. "Happy Birthday, Gordon, my love." She took a long drink, almost emptying the glass in one drought.

Gordon looked at her with something other than compassion in his eyes. "Drunk again." He snorted. "Lisa and her boyfriend will be here in an hour for my birthday party. I think they're bringing their brats. My friends and coworkers should be coming too. The last thing I want is for everyone to see you drunk." He looked at the knife and saw red liquid running down the edge of it. Some had spilled onto Margret's hand, giving her a murderous hue. "What are you doing with that?"

"We aren't having a party," she replied, her voice suddenly sober and her eyes focused. "Not today, not tomorrow." She looked at him with raised eyebrows. "I went to pick up your cake, but my card was declined." She drank the last of her wine. "The caterer for the banquet said you owed them money from the last two parties. She's been trying to call you for months. Glenda left dozens of messages, but you never called her back." Margret tossed the glass on the floor, and it shattered. "So, no party."

The phone in Gordon's pocket rang again. He took it out and looked at the name. "Again! Leave me alone. It's

Christmas Eve and my birthday!" he spat. He held the phone to his ear. "Stop calling me," he shouted. "I know. I know. I know. I'll pay you when I can."

Margret looked at him snidely. "Was that the bank? They've called twice today looking for you. I told them I hadn't seen you in two days." She bit her lip. "Unfortunately I didn't have to lie about that. Where've you been?"

He ignored her question. "What's with the knife?"

"Oh, this?" She held it up like a trophy. "Well, I had to improvise. When I learned we wouldn't have your party catered, I realized we needed a turkey." She lifted her shoulders playfully. "Happy birthday or merry Christmas, whichever you prefer."

"What did you do, you stupid drunk?" He disappeared into the house, and a minute later he screamed. "Margret!"

She made no effort to reply. Gordon thundered back into the room carrying a headless parrot. "You idiot." His lip curled. He enunciated every word with sharp clarity. "That bird cost twenty thousand dollars."

She blinked her eyes playfully. "The last time the bank called, I talked to them. Asked a few questions of my own." She dropped the knife, and it bounced on the tile floor. "You've spent every penny we have. You owe the bank, you owe credit cards that I didn't know about, you owe taxes and who knows what else." She got emotional, covering her mouth with her hand. "All for things you wanted. This house, that stupid car, the bird, your ridiculous parties. You get whatever you want, whenever you want it."

Her lip quivered. "Worst of all, you stole from your

children. That money was for them, and it's all gone. I can understand that you like to have your *whatever*, but at the expense of your children?" She rubbed her eyes like she was trying to wake up. "That money wasn't yours. It was a gift from your father! You squandered your inheritance *and* theirs."

Gordon looked around like he'd just remembered something. "Where are the kids?"

"Like you care," she spat.

"Margret," he shouted, his veins about to burst. "Where are the kids?" He threw the headless bird, and it bounced off her shoulder. She hardly flinched. Not satisfied with the damage he'd done with the parrot missile, he bent down and grabbed the knife. "Where are my children?"

"You never ask about *your* children," she accused. "I've sent them to your mother. I told her we have no money and nothing to offer them for Christmas this year because you spent everything we have. Merry Christmas, Gordon!"

Gordon's chest heaved in and out and his nostrils flared. He was a bull, ready to charge. His eyes glossed over, dull and vacant, like he wasn't in his right mind...like he was possessed.

"Spirit," Pemblin shouted. "I've seen enough." Pemblin willed the fog to cover the images of Gordi and Margret.

"You're worth less than my dead parrot," Gordi shouted. He lunged at her, the knife poised for delivery.

"Ebenezer! Take me away from here. I beg you. This can't be."

"It is, in fact, a shadow of that which is," Scrooge said.

Pemblin fell to his knees and held his hands like he was praying. "Please take me away from here." He cried openly, his face an image of torment. "Please, please."

He threw himself at Ebenezer's feet, and the hat tumbled off Pemblin's head. He held Scrooge's ankles and pleaded with his face flat on the ground.

Scrooge picked up the hat and put it on. "Pemblin," he said, "Your son does become something awful."

"But you said these are shadows of what the future could be. It's not solid yet, remember." Pemblin dripped emotion.

"The seeds of his character are planted, Mr. Pemblin. You can only do so much."

Pemblin wailed. "How do my other children fare? And I heard talk of my sweetheart. What of her?" Pemblin's voice was shaky. "And nothing of me but the inheritance I left . . . the inheritance which was squandered. I beg you. What does it mean?"

"It would be better if I could show you."

"No, no. I wish I was blind and dead of feeling. My daughters? My wife? Why am I not with them?"

"You died. We all have to. Your daughters marry and live like the rest of us," Scrooge comforted. "The sickness born in Gordon doesn't latch on to them as strongly, though it's there. You leave a fortune to your survivors, and they are taken care of for a long time. Yet, only Mrs. Pemblin has the discipline to make it last."

Thomas sobbed, and squeezed his eyes shut.

"You are a good man, Pemblin, when you die. No malice or evil in your heart. Your conscience is clear except for one point. Just one regret pings your soul."

"What is it, Ebeneezer? It's in regards to my children, isn't it? I can feel it in my bones. I fail them somehow."

"I cannot say, dear Mr. Pemblin. It is not my observation to reveal, as I am only a herald."

"Please," Pemblin cried, tears spilling down his cheeks. "Speak counsel to me. How can I change this future?"

"Thomas G. Pemblin." Scrooge's voice was all compassion. "Know ye the Ghost of Christmas Future? The Ghost of Christmas yet to come?"

"Is he here, Scrooge? Is he here that I should see him?"

"Indeed he is here." Scrooge lifted Pemblin's hand and helped him rise. "It is good that your eyes are closed, until you choose to see with them." Scrooge put his thumbs over Pemblin's eyes and wiped away the wetness. "Open, and see the Ghost of Christmas Yet to Come."

Pemblin opened his eyes. He was in his living room and Ebenezer stood before him. He looked behind Ebenezer, but saw no one. "You *are* the Ghost of Christmas Yet to Come, aren't you, Ebenezer Scrooge?"

Scrooge humbly shook his head. He looked at Pemblin, his eyes sparkling with Christmas magic. "Why you, Mr. Pemblin, you asked. Why have we come to visit you on this magical Christmas Eve?"

Pemblin searched for an answer, but had nothing.

"See me as I was on that Christmas Eve so many years ago, my heart and mind black as tar."

Thick chains broke through the ceiling, scattering wood and debris. They circled the room like snakes and clasped themselves around Ebenezer's wrists, holding him tight with iron bands. Like fountains erupting from the Earth, chains sprang from the ground and latched onto his feet, sending pieces of the broken floor hurling through the air. More chains burst through the windows, causing a cascade of glass to shower down on them. The chains wrapped around Scrooge's waist and shoulders. A giant black steel clamp bound itself around Scrooge's neck and latched shut, screws driven by an invisible hand. Ebenezer was pulled tight and lifted off the ground like he was about to be quartered.

His eyes, which seconds ago held the spark of Christmas, were hollow and dim, no pupils, only blackness. His voice became deep like a bull frog that croaked under water. "Chains! The chains of my choices. The chains of was."

Pemblin stared with wide and woeful eyes. "Why do you wear these? Your story and reformation are the embodiment of the Christmas spirit. If you can't shake these chains, who can? Are we all damned?"

Scrooge burst into flames. Pemblin fell to the floor and covered his face.

"Look at me," Scrooge commanded, his voice a cannonade of thunder. "Remove the hat from my head and place it on your own."

Pemblin, terrified and cowering, raised his eyes from the ground. He stood on wobbly knees and tried not to look at the burning Scrooge. Pemblin expected to catch fire any second.

"Look on me!" Scrooge's voice was a gunshot to Pemblin's ears. The flames, bright red and yellow, licked the walls and chains as they torched Scrooge. The heat enveloped

Pemblin's body. He knew he was dying. In the fire, Scrooge began to wither like a weed under celestial heat. "Take my hat!" he commanded.

Believing he was already doomed, Pemblin reached into the fire and grabbed the hat. He took a few steps back and put it on.

At once the flames disappeared and the chains clanked on the floor. The shackle around Scrooge's neck shattered into pieces, and the heavy bolts clanked to the floor. The shackles on his wrists and ankles disintegrated into powder, and Scrooge stepped free, no longer a prisoner. He did not return to the ground, but floated in the air. A thin layer of brilliant blue light glowed around him.

"Thomas, my friend." Scrooge's voice was pure and strong, the sound of distant thunder rolling on the wind. "See me now, my chains thrust aside. My arms and legs are unfettered so I may carry what I wish."

Scrooge descended to the floor and touched the chains with his foot. Immediately they shone as bright and blue as Scrooge himself. They rose off the ground and floated into Scrooge's outstretched hand. "These are the chains that would have damned me. Now I pull them with me by choice. They are the deeds which transformed my character. They are what connect me with those aided by my hand. Once they were the chains of the damned; now they are the links of love." He gathered the chains and placed them on his shoulders. "Thomas, my companion. These are the links of Christmas."

The light around Scrooge shone brighter and brighter, the blue melting into a brilliant white. Thomas thought the brightness would consume him, but it didn't. "Thomas, our hope. Know you now the Ghost of Christmas Yet to Come?"

Somehow the answer was given to him, and he did know. "Me, Ebenezer. I am the Ghost of Christmas Yet to Come. I am the Ghost of Christmas Future."

"It is so."

"Am I dead?" Thomas asked.

"There is life in you yet. Fear not death. Fear life without Christmas."

"How am I to be a herald for the season while still living?" Pemblin asked.

But Scrooge and his chains had vanished.

CHRISTMAS MORNING

Once again, Pemblin was standing in his bedroom next to the window. His face was no longer wet with tears. No fire or glowing blue light penetrated his eyes. He looked at his wife, still sleeping in bed. "Christmas magic," he said, knowing she wouldn't hear him.

She stirred. "Thomas? Is everything all right?" She sat up and looked at the alarm clock. "It's four in the morning. Are the kids awake?"

"Everything is fine, dear."

"Why are you out of bed?" She wiped her eyes. "And why are you wearing that hat?"

He'd forgotten about Scrooge's hat. He took it off and looked at it. Glossy black felt with a thick red ribbon around the stock. Just over the front left side was a holly blossom. He laughed. "Merry Christmas, my love."

Pemblin switched on his bedside lamp, sat next to Mrs. Pemblin, and told her everything. From the moment he heard the voice on the walkway, to the moment he met Ebenezer Scrooge, to when he saw the Ghost of Christmas Present dragged away by wolves. For Thomas, there was no one more trustworthy than Mrs. Pemblin, and he told her without doubting she'd believe. Such was the man that Thomas G. Pemblin had been to her. An honest man. A good man.

"And this is the hat Scrooge left me." He held it up.

"But Thomas," she questioned, "what are you supposed to do?"

"Live, my dear. Live and be happy." He sprang off the bed and grabbed both her hands. "And teach our children to do the same." He pulled her toward the door. "Come with me."

They stood by the tree and admired the rainbow of lights. Stockings hung from the mantle, filled with miscellaneous joys, and Santa's cookies were gone. All was how it should be. "Great," he said. "Now we wait."

It didn't take long. Pemblin heard footsteps on the stairs, and then he saw little Jillian's head peak around the corner. Lisa was right behind her. They saw the new gifts under the tree, and their eyes grew large. Lisa smiled and clapped her hands with joy. Pemblin knew what was going to happen because he'd seen it with the Ghost of Christmas Present. He watched as Jillian and Lisa checked the cookies and the reindeer food.

But Pemblin did not see himself walk into the room or rub his belly. He was already there, and he'd already rubbed it. Instead, Lisa and Jillian ran upstairs and declared to Gordi that Christmas morning had come. Pemblin heard the thumping of feet overhead. All three children entered the room, their eyes so captivated by the blaring lights and new gifts that they didn't notice their mom and dad sitting on the couch.

"Stockings!" Gordi exclaimed. He reached for the one with his name stitched on it.

"Merry Christmas," Mr. Pemblin said.

Gordi jumped. "Dad!" He covered his chest. "You scared me." He saw his mother. "What are you guys doing down here?"

"It's Christmas for us too." Mr. Pemblin couldn't suppress his smile.

"I know, but isn't it early?" Gordi shrugged. "Adults do the sleeping thing, right?"

Pemblin nodded. "We usually do, don't we. I want to try something different."

Pemblin gathered his family, and before one person touched a present for themselves or anyone else, they gave thanks. Thanks for life, for the season, for each other, for Christmas, and for the Author of it all.

After all the packages had been opened and thanks had been shared, they sat in the living room and talked of their new treasures and of the wonderful day to come.

Except Gordon. He sat away from them, his head bowed low over his new phone.

"Gordi, put that away, please. I didn't get you that so I would never see your face again."

"But Dad, it's mine, and I'm just getting used to it," he whined. "It's my favorite present."

"You can do that later. I want you to come over here and be a part of the family." He beckoned with his head. "Over here."

"No thanks, I'm good right here." Gordi swiped a finger across the phone.

Pemblin jumped up and snatched the phone from Gordon's hand.

"Hey! That's mine," Gordon protested.

Pemblin looked stern. "I love you, Gordi. But I won't tolerate your disrespect." He walked to the nearest bathroom with Gordon fast on his heels. Without hesitation, he lifted the toilet seat and dropped the phone in the water. It made a splash that spilled on the floor. He pointed to the toilet. "Our relationship is worth more than a thousand dollars." He pulled Gordi into a mandatory hug. "That's what I paid for your broken phone."

"Mom," Gordon said, speaking quietly and pointing to the toilet bowl. "Dad doesn't know its waterproof, does he?"

She laughed. "I suppose not. But mind your father, Gordi."

Pemblin looked in the toilet. "Waterproof? I need one of those." He stared at Gordi, trying to find the entitled, irresponsible and murderous man hidden in those ten-year-old eyes. He couldn't.

"Gordi," Pemblin said. "The phone is mine now. If you want it, you have to earn it back."

"Yeah, funny Dad." Gordon rolled his eyes.

Mr. Pemblin locked eyes with his son. "I mean it." Gordon reached for the phone, but Mr. Pemblin blocked him.

Gordon drew desperate, realizing that he wasn't going to win. He crossed his arms and stomped his foot. "But it's my birthday present!" he cried, tears rolling down his face.

"You will have to earn it." Pemblin was immovable. "We don't just get stuff because it's our birthday or Christmas. You aren't entitled to anything."

Gordi was defeated. He sobbed. "What's entitled?"

Mr. Pemblin pulled him close again. He looked at Denise over their son's head. "I know it's a big word for a ten-year-old. I'm not sure I even understand it. We can figure it out together. For now, it means you need to earn the things that come to you." He broke the hug and held Gordi at arm's length. "And we will start with that phone. Understand?"

Looking none too pleased, Gordi nodded and wiped his eyes. "Whose hat?" He pointed over his father's shoulder.

Scrooge's hat lay at the bottom of the stairs. "Oh! It's mine," Pemblin said as he picked it up.

He admired the hat. It definitely wasn't fashionable by the day's standards, but it had a rustic beauty to it. The shape and posh design, the black felt, red ribbon and holly berry all contributed to its aesthetic appeal. But for Pemblin, the hat was a symbol, a reminder of a Christmas Eve night that was full of wonder. Ceremoniously, he placed it on his head.

Suddenly, he had the strongest urge to run into the street. He was disturbed by the sheer absurdity of it. Stronger and stronger the urge became until he could no longer fight it.

He ran out the front door and down the snow covered walkway in his bare feet. He opened the gate, which the wolves of Christmas Present had almost knocked over. The snow under his feet was cold and crunchy. He stopped in the middle of the road.

"Honey," Mrs. Pemblin yelled as she stood in the doorway. "You okay?"

He wasn't sure. A car pulled onto the street and drove his direction. Pemblin wanted to move, but something inside him, some invisible compass, told him to stay. The thought crossed his mind that if he was going to be the Ghost of Christmas Yet to Come, then he would need to be a ghost. Death by car and on Christmas day. Dead. He thought he'd have more time.

"Thomas!" Mrs. Pemblin shouted. "Get out of the road!" The children gathered around her at the door.

The car did not run him over. Instead, it pulled next to him, and the driver's side window rolled down. "Good morning and merry Christmas," Alvin said. "Nice hat."

"Alvi!" Pemblin shouted.

Alvin looked surprised. He turned to his wife in the passenger seat. "Did you tell him to call me that?"

Pemblin ducked his head so he could see in the car. Mrs. York shook her head and laughed.

"Kids," Pemblin shouted. "Come and meet one of the greatest business minds of our day." He waved them over. "You too, Denise," he said to Mrs. Pemblin.

"Mr. and Mrs. York," Pemblin tried to put his arms around his family, "this is Gordon, Lisa and Jillian. And I'm sure you know Denise."

Mrs. York leaned over. "Hi, kids. I see you guys playing all the time. It's a shame we don't know each other well. Imagine that." She rested a hand on her husband's arm. "We've lived here for three years, and this is the first we've had a proper greeting with the . . ." she lost her words. "Good gracious." She covered her mouth. "I don't even know your last name."

"Pemblin," Thomas said. "We are the Pemblins. And

Denise and I were wondering if you'd join us for dinner tonight. It's Christmas, so we'll have it a little early, but it's always a feast. How does four o'clock sound?"

"Thomas," Mrs. Pemblin chided. She adjusted her robe, looking a little uncomfortable in her pajamas. "Don't put them on the spot like that. Where are your manners?"

"Oh, it's quite all right, Mrs. Pemblin," Alvin consoled. "We appreciate the invite, but we're on our way to a little work celebration. I don't know what time we'll be back. . . ."

"But we'll be there," Mrs. York interrupted. She looked happily at Jillian and Lisa, who both held a Christmas toy in their arms. "What should we bring?"

Mrs. Pemblin took the change in her schedule with such civility that you'd think it had always been in her mind. "Nothing. Just yourselves." She looked at her husband. "Thomas is right; it's always a feast for just the five of us. We eat leftovers for days."

"All right, then," Pemblin said. "Back inside with you all. Don't want anyone to catch cold." He shooed the children back to the house.

"Gordi," he yelled. "Grab a shovel and clear off Mr. Hartwick's walkway, please. He did it himself yesterday, but it snowed all night. Make sure you tell him merry Christmas when you're done."

Gordi groaned, but walked to the garage where Mr. Pemblin kept the shovel.

"Well, I guess we'll see you later," Alvin said as he put the car in drive. He started to pull away when Pemblin put his hand on the car's open window.

"Oh. I forgot to ask." Pemblin did his best to sound unrehearsed, like he had no insights into the life of Alvin York. Alvin had power to influence the lives of millions of people, so Pemblin wanted to say something meaningful. Something that could mean more, but sound like less.

"Alvi." It was Pemblin's lips that moved, it was his mouth that formed the words, but it was not his voice that Alvin York heard. It was a voice more tender and deeper than Pemblin's, at least to Alvin.

Alvin looked at Pemblin but didn't see him. He was getting off the bus and running with his friend across the street. He was crying because Santa Claus wasn't real. "Alvi," his father repeated. "If there is no Santa Claus, does that mean there is no Christmas?"